RULES OF THE
DEATH GAME

"Have you ever been in a sash fight before, *Señor* Fargo?" Chavez asked with a sharklike relish.

"No," Fargo said.

"You pick up your end of the sash and stick it in your mouth," the Comanchero leader explained. "Black Bear will do the same at his end. Then you both pick up your Bowies and fight. There are only two rules, *amigo*. You must not let the sash drop from your mouth, and you must not leave the circle—or else my men will kill you on the spot."

Fargo looked around the circle of Comancheros. Their dark eyes were lit with blood lust. His blood. He looked at his opponent. Black Bear was bursting with confidence. He was an expert at this game that Fargo had never played before.

Fargo knew that the odds were bad. Even worse was if he came out on top, he would be torn apart by the angry onlookers. What the hell, thought the Trailsman as he bit down hard on the blood-red sash and tightened his grip on the hilt of the razor-sharp Bowie, he'd just as soon go out a winner. . . .

THE TRAILSMAN

155

OKLAHOMA ORDEAL

by

Jon Sharpe

A SIGNET BOOK

SIGNET
Published by the Penguin Group
Penguin Books USA Inc., 375 Hudson Street,
New York, New York 10014, U.S.A.
Penguin Books Ltd, 27 Wrights Lane,
London W8 5TZ, England
Penguin Books Australia Ltd, Ringwood,
Victoria, Australia
Penguin Books Canada Ltd, 10 Alcorn Avenue,
Toronto, Ontario, Canada M4V 3B2
Penguin Books (N.Z.) Ltd, 182–190 Wairau Road,
Auckland 10, New Zealand

Penguin Books Ltd, Registered Offices:
Harmondsworth, Middlesex, England

First published by Signet,
an imprint of Dutton Signet,
a division of Penguin Books USA Inc.

First Printing, November, 1994
10 9 8 7 6 5 4 3 2 1

The first chapter of this book previously appeared in *Ambush at Skull Pass*, the one
hundred fifty-fourth volume in this series.

  REGISTERED TRADEMARK—MARCA REGISTRADA

Printed in the United States of America

The Trailsman

Beginnings . . . they bend the tree and they mark the man. Skye Fargo was born when he was eighteen. Terror was his midwife, vengeance his first cry. Killing spawned Skye Fargo, ruthless, cold-blooded murder. Out of the acrid smoke of gunpowder still hanging in the air, he rose, cried out a promise never forgotten.

The Trailsman they began to call him all across the West: searcher, scout, hunter, the man who could see where others only looked, his skills for hire but not his soul, the man who lived each day to the fullest, yet trailed each tomorrow. Skye Fargo, the Trailsman, and the seeker who could take the wildness of a land and the wanting of a woman and make them his own.

1860, border country
—where men rode at their own risk,
and women were fair game...

tor missed and went sailing past. Whirling, Fargo swept his

1

At first Skye Fargo thought the keening sound he heard was the wind. A storm loomed on the western horizon, and already the breeze had picked up to the point where it imitated a banshee. But when the mournful wail was repeated, he knew instantly the sound came from a human throat.

Reining up, the big man rose in the stirrups of his pinto stallion and surveyed the rolling prairie on either side of the rutted trail he followed. Other than the rippling of the grass there was no hint of movement, no trace of another human being.

Fargo pushed his white hat back on his head and idly scratched his chin. He was too seasoned a plainsman for his ears to be playing tricks on him. There had to be someone out there, someone in trouble. And judging by the scream, that someone was a woman.

Clucking the Ovaro forward, Fargo slowly rode to the southwest, loosening his Colt in its holster as a sensible precaution. A lone rider never knew when trouble might rear its unwanted head, either from hostile Indians, savage beasts, or outlaws whose savagery made the beasts seem tame by comparison.

Suddenly, the cry was repeated a third time. Fargo pinpointed the direction, due north, and lightly applied his spurs to the stallion's flanks. He shucked the pistol, holding it close to his thigh.

The prairie could be deceptive. A man might think it went on forever, flat and unchanged mile after mile, when in truth a gully or ravine or dry wash might be a stone's throw away. This time it was the latter, sixty yards from the trail.

Fargo heard muffled voices and slowed to a walk so he wouldn't advertise his presence. His sharp eyes saw where a wagon had crushed the grass within the past hour or so as the vehicle rolled to the gently sloping rim of the wash, then down on over. Halting, he slid off and padded closer to investigate.

A wagon of the sort favored by drummers rested at the bottom, its team standing at rest. Nearby were six people. Three hardcases ringed an older man in a faded black suit and black derby who was flat on his back with blood trickling from one corner of his mouth. A pair of young women stood to one side, both pretty fillies blessed by nature with the sort of fine looks that made Fargo's blood race and his mouth go dry.

As Fargo watched, a blond woman launched herself at a string bean of a man, screeching, "You leave him alone, damn you!"

Quick as a panther, the man whirled, catching hold of both her wrists before she could pummel him. "Calm down, missy," he snapped. "This old geezer has this comin', and he's going to take his licks whether you like it or not."

"You have no call to be doing this to our pa!" declared the other woman, a brunette whose curly locks cascaded to the small of her slender back.

"I reckon we do," said another man, nudging her father with the toe of his boot. "This bastard should of gotten his due a long time ago."

"We'll report you to the law!" countered the brunette.

Two of the men chuckled, and the string bean shoved the blonde from him. "Go right ahead, ma'am," he said. "I'm sure any lawdog in the territory would be mighty interested in your doings."

The third hombre, a grizzled hardcase whose steely eyes glittered with spite, bent down to roughly haul the older man erect. "Enough jawing," he barked. "It's time we got down to business. I got me a hankering to reach Guthrie by nightfall." Without warning he slammed a fist into the old man's gut, doubling him over.

"Damn you!" cried the brunette, springing to her father's defense. She was seized by the second man.

The blonde promptly tried once more to intervene and was again grabbed by String Bean, who commented, "Do what we came for, Jeb. These ladies won't be botherin' you none."

Fargo saw Jeb punch the old man in the stomach a second time. When the father sank to his knees, sputtering, Fargo stood, leveled the Colt, and cocked the hammer. The metallic click caused the three hardcases to glance up sharply.

"Who the hell are you?" String Bean blurted.

"What do you want?" demanded Jeb.

Fargo wagged his pistol at three horses ground-hitched a score of feet down the wash. "I want you to mount up and head out."

"This ain't none of your affair," String Bean said.

"That's right," chimed in Jeb. "We won't take it kindly if you stick your nose in where it don't belong."

"I don't care how you take it," Fargo said, advancing carefully down the incline. "Just so you leave before my trigger finger twitches."

String Bean released the blonde. "Are you with this bunch?" he asked angrily. "If so, I'm warnin' you here and now that you're askin' for a heap of grief."

The third man nodded as he pushed the brunette. "That's the gospel truth, mister. We look out after our own. There'll be hell to pay for what's been done."

"There'll be hell to pay if you don't fork leather," Fargo warned, tiring of their empty threats.

Scowling, the trio backed toward their mounts. Jeb dragged his heels, his right hand poised above his six-shooter, fingers clawed, twitching eagerly.

"I'd think twice if I was you," Fargo stated. To emphasize his point he slanted the Colt and stroked the trigger.

Jeb uttered a yelp, clutching his right ear. When he lowered his hand, there was blood on his fingers. "You son of a bitch!" he roared. "You shot my ear off!"

"I only nicked it," Fargo said. "And if you're not out of here in one minute, I'll aim a couple of inches to the left."

Grumbling and glaring, the three climbed on their horses. At the top of the wash they each looked back, hatred lining their features, especially Jeb's. String Bean voiced a whoop, and all three galloped off in a cloud of dust.

Skye Fargo began reloading his six-gun in case they returned. The drum of hoofbeats gradually receded, fading in due course to silence. Only then did the women and the old man stir to life.

"Thank heaven you came to our rescue, sir!" the blonde

said. "There's no telling what those ruffians would have done to our poor pa."

"We can never thank you enough," added the brunette.

"I'm sure you could if you tried," Fargo responded, grinning and meeting her frank gaze with a suggestive look.

Their father coughed and touched his split lip. "I daresay this sort of thing is all too common on the frontier. A man in my profession is always treated shabbily by the rougher element." Extending his arm, he said, "But enough about those scalawags. Where are my manners? I'm Phinneas T. Boggs, at your service, my good man. And these lovelies are my daughters, Liberty"—he gestured at the blonde—"and Belle." He nodded at the brunette.

"You're pulling my leg," Fargo said.

"Never, sir," Phinneas replied. "Ask anyone. A lie has never passed these lips." He removed his derby and wiped a sleeve across his perspiring brow. "My wife, bless her departed soul, was from Philadelphia. Patriotic to the core, she was." Phinneas smirked. "Actually, I should count my blessings she didn't name our girls Betsy and Ross."

The spent cartridge replaced, Fargo twirled the Colt into his holster.

Liberty whistled. "You're right handy with that shooting iron, aren't you?"

"I've had some practice," Fargo allowed. He glanced at the wagon and for the first time noticed the words painted on the wooden side. "Phinneas Boggs," he read aloud. "Miracle cures for every ailment."

"No idle boast," Phinneas said proudly. "I've plied my trade for nigh thirty years now. There isn't a sickness I haven't treated, an injury I haven't fixed."

"You're a patent medicine man," Fargo said, abruptly suspicious. Patent medicine men were notorious throughout the West as the biggest liars and cheats in all creation. They traveled from town to town, offering to cure everything under the sun, but many of their so-called medicines turned out to be worthless concoctions that often did their patients more harm than good. He stared in the direction taken by the hardcases, wondering.

The older man squared his shoulders. "That I am," he declared. "And I can tell by your face what you're thinking. But you misjudge me, sir. There are thousands of grateful people from here to the Mississippi who will testify to my ability and integrity."

"What about those men?" Fargo asked. "Did you sell them some of your medicine?"

"As God is my witness, no," Phinneas said gravely.

"All my pa did was stand up to them when they tried to take advantage of Liberty and me," Belle said.

"That's right," her sister agreed. "They wanted to buy us drinks back in Guthrie, and when we refused, they took it badly. So the vermin followed us all this way. Not ten minutes ago they forced pa to drive off the trail so no one would interfere while they did as they pleased."

"Only you saved us," Liberty breathed, brazenly taking hold of Fargo's arm and giving it a gentle squeeze. She studied his whipcord frame, the pink tip of her tongue poking between her cherry lips.

"You wouldn't happen to be on your way to Rawbone, would you?" Phinneas inquired.

Fargo was on his way to Texas where he had an appointment with a man who wanted to hire him to track down a band of cutthroats responsible for murdering the man's family. Rawbone lay on his route, not twenty miles farther. "I'll be passing through," he revealed.

"Excellent!" Phinneas said. "In that case, perhaps you'd consent to ride with us the rest of the way? It would put my mind at ease knowing my daughters had such a capable protector."

Liberty squealed in delight and squeezed Fargo harder. "Oh, please do! We haven't had anyone else to talk to for three days."

"You won't regret it," Belle added.

The promise in her tone was unmistakable. Fargo admired the tantalizing swell of her hips and how nicely the brunette filled out her blouse. His manhood twitched, reminding him of the week and a half he'd just spent in the saddle, a week and a half without female companionship. "I'd be happy to ride with you," he said.

"How wonderful!" Liberty exclaimed, impulsively pecking Fargo on the cheek. At a look from her father she let go of the big man's arm and stepped back, bowing her head in apparent embarrassment at her behavior.

"You'll have to excuse my girls," Phinneas said. "Sometimes they're too darn friendly for their own good."

"I don't mind," Fargo said, thinking that they couldn't possibly reach Rawbone before the next afternoon, which meant he'd be spending all night in the company of the two lovelies. There were worse fates.

"Fine," the father said. "Give me a few minutes to get my wagon back on level ground, and we'll be on our way."

Nodding, Fargo headed up the slope toward the Ovaro. His head cleared the rim, then his shoulders. He mentally pictured both sisters buck naked with him lying between them, and smirked. Distracted by his lust, he didn't notice the distant glint of sunlight off metal until it was almost too late. He threw himself down as a lead hornet buzzed by, and a split second later the crack of a rifle shot rippled across the grassland.

"Damn!" Phinneas cried. "They're still after us!"

Fargo had the Colt out. Removing his hat, he rose high enough to take a hasty peek. He couldn't see the shooter, but he knew the man was about sixty yards out, to the west. One of the men, at least, had doubled back. If all three had, he was trapped.

"How dare they!" Liberty said. Dainty fists clenched, she stormed up the slope. "I've had my fill of these jackasses!"

Before the foolish young woman could expose herself, Fargo grabbed a shapely ankle and pulled, upending her on her backside next to him. She let out an indignant squawk, then slapped at his hand.

"What do you think you're doing?"

"Saving your hide," Fargo said.

"They wouldn't shoot a woman," Liberty protested, trying to jerk her leg free.

"They'll put a bullet into anything that moves," Fargo said. Releasing her, he picked up a hefty rock, rolled onto his side, and hurled the rock skyward. Immediately a pair of rifles blasted. The rock shattered, sharp fragments raining down on Fargo and the woman, causing her to flinch. He stared at her and she turned beet red.

"Sorry, mister. My anger got the better of me."

14

Phinneas, bent low, joined them. "What can we do? We're pinned down, completely at their mercy."

"I say we fight," Belle declared, moving toward the rear of the wagon. "We've let them push us around long enough." She yanked open a small door and disappeared inside.

Inching upward, Fargo checked on his pinto. The loyal Ovaro was a dozen feet off, exactly where he had left it, patiently awaiting his return. He had to get the animal under cover, and quickly. Inserting two fingers into his mouth, he whistled softly twice. The stallion lifted its head, ears pricked, and swiftly advanced.

Fargo took a calculated gamble to distract the three men from the pinto. Rising on his knees, he fired three times, fanning the pistol. He shifted after each shot, sending a slug to the west, south, and north. There were no targets visible, but that didn't matter. He only wanted to draw their attention and he succeeded admirably.

A ragged volley blistered the rim, slugs punching into the dirt from several directions at once. Fargo ducked down, a reaction the three men would be expecting. But then he did the unexpected; he vaulted from concealment, bounded to the Ovaro, seized the reins, and spun, intending to reach safety before the trio recovered from their surprise and cut loose. In this he failed, for as he turned, he spied String Bean to the north, already upright and taking deliberate aim with a Henry. The range was too great for a revolver. For an instant Fargo stared death in the face, the short hairs at the nape of his neck prickling.

A new element was added when another gun thundered before String Bean could fire. Belle had popped up, a rifle tucked to her shoulder. Her shot drove String Bean to ground, buying Fargo the precious seconds needed for him to scoot into the wash. He barely made it when the hardcases peppered the rim.

Belle had flattened and was feeding another cartridge into her rifle. She winked at Fargo and said,"I think I winged him. I would have done better, but I rushed on your account."

"I'm grateful," Fargo said. From his saddle scabbard he took his Sharps. Making certain it was loaded, he glided over to her. "Where did you learn to shoot like that?"

"I was a regular tomboy when I was younger," Belle explained rather sheepishly. "At an age when most other girls were playing with dolls or helping their mothers around the house, I was off hunting and fishing. Now pa counts on me to supply game for the table whenever we're on the go."

Fargo moved past her to the top. Using his thumb he cocked the Sharps, then pulled the rear trigger to set the front trigger for the slightest of pressure. The three hardcases were nowhere to be seen, but he doubted they had gone, not when they wanted to get their hands on the sisters badly enough to kill anyone who stood in their way.

Going prone, Fargo wedged the heavy rifle to his shoulder. He held the barrel low to the ground to reduce the gleam of sunshine off the metal surface. Elbows firmly propped, he scanned the wash, which was cast in shadow by oncoming storm clouds. The wind had intensified even more, bringing with it the dank scent of moisture.

"This is all we need!" Phinneas remarked, regarding the overcast western sky with annoyance.

Fargo shifted to inform Boggs that the rain might work in their favor. He happened to spy a lanky figure fifty yards out, darting from north to east. Instantly, he swiveled, swinging the Sharps as he turned. A hasty bead had to suffice, and then he stroked the trigger.

Arms flapping, the figure twisted and flew backward to vanish in high weeds.

"Did you get one?" Belle asked hopefully.

"Maybe," Fargo said, reloading.

Gunfire erupted from two directions, a senseless fusillade that spewed geysers of dirt from the rim.

"They're mad as wet hens," Belle said gleefully. "You must have made wolf meat of one of the buzzards."

Gradually, the shooting died off, and for several minutes all was quiet until the rumble of far off thunder heralded strong gusts of wind and a light spattering of rain drops.

Phinneas and Liberty scooted over, the father saying anxiously, "What do you suggest we do? They can slip in here under cover of the storm and pick us off one by one."

"That works both ways," Fargo said, indicating the wagon. "I want you to get set to move on out like a bat out of hell when I give the word."

"Is that wise? My wagon is too heavy to take this slope very

16

fast," Phinneas hedged. "We'll be like clay targets in a shooting gallery."

"Not if I keep them busy," Fargo stated in a tone that made it clear he was in no mood for an argument.

"But if something should happen to my dear daughters . . . ," Phinneas said, leaving the thought unfinished.

"You were the one who asked for my help, remember?" Fargo reminded him. "Either we do this my way or you can fend for yourselves."

Reluctantly, the older man hastened to the wagon. Belle and Liberty squeezed onto the seat beside him, Belle on the outside so she could use her rifle if need be.

Bigger drops of rain were falling. Fargo tilted his head, letting the cool moisture dampen his face while he marked the position of the leading bank of clouds. Timing would be critical. Too soon, and the hardcases would cut them down before they covered twenty yards. Too late, and the rain would be so heavy Boggs wouldn't be able to see a foot in front of his face and might flip the wagon.

Retrieving his hat, Fargo dashed to the Ovaro, stepped into the stirrups, and bent over the saddle horn so the three men wouldn't catch sight of him. He slid the Sharps into the scabbard, then palmed the Colt.

With each passing minute the din of clashing thunder grew louder. Piercing lightning bolts cleaved the heavens. The drizzle increased, becoming a steady downpour. And the whole time the sky became darker, ever darker.

The patent medicine man had the look of a man on the verge of unbridled panic. Phinneas held the reins so tightly his knuckles were pale and he repeatedly licked his dry lips. His dark eyes were wide, his face caked with sweat.

By contrast, the sisters were surprisingly composed, Belle wearing a determined expression, Liberty aglow with excitement. Neither showed any fear.

Fargo decided the time was right. "Now!" he bellowed, beckoning with his gun hand. Phinneas hesitated, too scared to obey, until prompted into action by Belle who jammed an elbow into his ribs.

Lashing the reins, Phinneas brought the team to a lumbering start. The bottom of the wash was just wide enough for a tight turn. A muleskinner could have made it with ease, but Phinneas was no muleskinner. He worked hard, fighting his balking animals, giving them a taste of his small whip.

It was obvious the man needed help. A jab of Fargo's heels brought the pinto close to the team. Bending sideways, Fargo gripped the bridle of the near horse and tugged, guiding it to the spot on the slope where the wagon could climb without much difficulty.

A tremendous clap of thunder caused both horses to shy and whinny. The wagon skidded backward a few feet. Phinneas half rose, applying the lash of his whip with a vengeance. The team lunged forward, muscles rippling, hoofs digging deep into the now slick earth.

Fargo stayed close to them. The wagon reached the incline, and he saw the wagon wheels lose traction. He worried that he had waited too long and gave the near horse a slap on the flank that had no effect.

A jagged shaft of lightning proved to be their salvation. It struck so close, his scalp tingled and provoked the team into redoubling its efforts. Slowly, foot by foot, the wagon scaled the wash. The off wheel hit a large rock halfway up, making the whole wagon pitch like a boat in a gale. Liberty had to clutch the corner to keep from being thrown off.

Fargo pulled ahead a few yards. His head cleared the rise, and all he saw were driving sheets of rain, which was as he hoped would be the case. Behind him the wagon rattled noisily, but he was confident the noise was drowned out by the shrieking wind. He cleared the wash and paused to let the wagon catch up.

At that moment another vivid bolt briefly illuminated the scene, and in its glow Skye Fargo beheld the hardcase named Jeb not twenty feet away, holding a leveled rifle.

2

For a frozen heartbeat neither man moved. Then Fargo and Jeb fired at the same time the very second the brief flare of light died out. Fargo wasn't hit, and he had no idea whether his aim had been any better. The pelting rain reduced visibility to a couple of yards at best.

The wagon clattered alongside him. Fargo waved Boggs on, and as the team broke into a gallop so did he. Neither Jeb nor either of the other men showed themselves.

The patent medicine man fled pell-mell across the drenched prairie. Fargo fell in behind the wagon to cover them. A minute elapsed, but there was no sign of pursuit. Convinced the ruse had worked, he galloped abreast of the team and shouted, "You can slow down some!" A thunderclap competed with his warning, and Phinneas Boggs seemed not to hear.

"Slow down!" Fargo stressed. "You're liable to have an accident!"

Belle turned and said something to her father, who shook his head. She reached for the reins and had her hand swatted aside. Glancing at Fargo, she gestured as if to say, "I tried."

"Damn it all," Fargo muttered. He swung the stallion closer to the front seat, then had to jerk on the reins to avoid a collision when the wagon unaccountably swerved.

"Phinneas!" Fargo roared, wasting his breath. The wagon hurtled onward, Boggs oblivious to all except his fright.

Fargo gave chase, jamming the Colt into his holster. The wind tore at him, threatening to blow off his hat. His buckskins were fast becoming soaked, and several drops trickled down his back. He was careful not to get too close to the wagon. Another mistake on Boggs's part might cost him his life.

The wagon raced recklessly onward. It jolted at every bump, shook at every rut. From inside rose a rattling racket as things crashed about.

Fargo came even with the rear panel. He tried to gauge the direction they were going, but it was hopeless. Thankfully, the plain was flat in that area, and he began to think they would be all right when the wagon gave a shuddering reel to the left with a loud splintering crash. It had gone over a short drop-off of three or four feet. Not high, but the damage had been done.

Phinneas was hauling on the reins as Fargo rode close enough to see the shattered spokes on the front wheel. The wagon slewed to a halt, and Fargo reined up, jumping down before the stallion stopped. He ran up to the seat and glared at the trembling Boggs. "What the hell did you think you were doing? Didn't you hear me?"

"Sorry!" Phinneas whined. "I don't know what got into me."

"We're stuck here until we can fix your spokes," Fargo said angrily, glancing around. Although he figured they had eluded the hardcases, he was not one to take anything for granted.

Belle twisted to open the door behind the seat, saying, "If that's the case, we should get in out of this rain. Come on in and I'll lend you a towel."

"You go," Fargo said. "Someone should keep watch for a while." He tied the reins to the broken wheel as Liberty and her father entered, then he pulled out the Sharps and climbed up. The roof of the wagon protruded well past the seat, shielding him from the worst of the downpour.

Belle had slid over to make room for him. She patted the seat and quipped, "Plant it there, handsome. I'll keep you company."

"There's no need," Fargo said.

"True. But I *want* to," Belle said, smiling warmly. Enough rain had fallen on her dress to mold the wet fabric to her legs, outlining the enticing contours of her thighs. "And don't fret. I'm tough. I won't catch my death of cold."

"I hope not," Fargo responded, making no attempt to hide the glint of sexual hunger in his eyes.

The brunette studied him, then nodded. "Most men like to

hide their true feelings all the time. Not you. You come straight to the point. I like that."

A yellow glow filled the doorway as a lantern was lit within. Phinneas vented a curse. "Look at this mess! It'll take a week of Sundays to clean!"

"It's not all that bad, Pa," Liberty said.

Fargo had to agree with her father. He looked in and discovered scores of small bottles, jars, and metal canisters lying in scattered piles on the floor, many with their contents partially spilled. Additional containers lined a dozen small racks affixed to the walls, most lying on their side or in jumbled clusters.

Phinneas caught Fargo's look and gestured sadly. "My medicines, sir. Or, to be more precise, the varied special ingredients I use in my concoctions. Some are quite rare, incapable of being replaced." Sinking to his knees, he commenced scooping dried leaves into his left hand. "This is awful. Just awful."

"We'll help you, Pa, as always," Liberty said, placing a hand on his slumped shoulder.

Her father gazed at her tenderly. "Where would I be without my precious girls? When things are gloomiest, you bring sunshine into my life."

A gust of wind suddenly fanned the interior, stirring the leaves and other items. Phinneas gave a start and said, "If you don't mind, sir," and shut the door.

"You'll have to excuse my father," Belle told Fargo. "His medicines mean everything to him. He's not like those charlatans who try to pass off watered-down whiskey mixed with rattlesnake venom as real cures."

"I'm glad to hear it," Fargo said, recalling an incident a few years back where another patent medicine man had been run out of a frontier town on a rail. "Being tarred and feathered is more painful than most realize."

"My father is legitimate, Mr. . . . ," Belle said and blinked. "Say. You haven't told us your name yet."

He did.

"Fargo," Belle repeated, rolling the word on her tongue as she might a piece of hard candy. "Not a name you hear every day. It fits you, though." She sidled closer and their shoulders touched. "Is there a Mrs. Fargo hid away some-where?"

"No. And if I have my way there never will be."

"Do tell." Belle chuckled. "There you go again. Laying all your cards on the table."

During their conversation the rain had begun to slacken, the thunder to taper off. At that juncture the sky convulsed one final time, the blast of the thunderclap so loud it rang in their ears. Belle acted spooked and jumped, and in so doing she nearly sat in Fargo's lap. Her face wound up inches from his, her lips so near Fargo could see the tiny wrinkles in them. Warm, minty breath caressed his skin.

"Goodness, that was too close for comfort!" Belle said huskily.

"It was just right," Fargo replied, gently pressing his mouth to hers. She yielded, her silken tongue meeting his, and he let the kiss linger, savoring the sensation. They were both breathing heavily when they parted for air.

"Ummmmm, nice," Belle commented, her features those of a cat that had just eaten a canary.

"There's a lot more where that came from," Fargo promised. "Whenever you're inclined."

Belle bobbed a chin at the door. "Don't let my poor pa hear you or he'll have a conniption. He thinks his daughters are pillars of virtue." She snickered. "Actually, Liberty and I lost ours years ago. But we're not hussies, you understand. We're just normal, healthy women, and we happen to be fond of handsome men. What's wrong with that?"

"You're asking the wrong man," Fargo said.

"Pa would see red if he ever caught us," Belle remarked. "Which has puzzled me considerably over the years. Why is it, do you reckon, that parents always expect their young ones to be so much more virtuous than they were themselves at the same age? Doesn't make a whole lot of sense to me."

"Few things in this life do."

"Is that the voice of experience speaking?" Belle wondered, leaning close again, her face upturned invitingly.

Fargo was about to embrace her when the door was yanked inward, framing Liberty. The blonde grinned impishly and poked her sister.

"Pa wants you to help out too, Belle, or we'll never get this darn mess cleaned up."

Sighing in disappointment, Belle nodded and went in, winking at Fargo as she did.

By now the rain was a light drizzle. Fargo peered around the corner and saw no evidence of the hardcases. Nor were there any landmarks he could use to orient himself. With the sky still densely overcast, he couldn't rely on the sun. His best guess was that Boggs had fled on a southeasterly course from the wash instead of to the southwest toward Rawbone, and that they couldn't have covered more than a mile or two before the wheel broke.

Swinging down, Fargo untied the reins and mounted. Backtracking was easy thanks to the fresh ruts that had only been partially wiped out by the heavy rain. In due course he came to where the wagon had crossed the main trail. Hand on his Colt, he warily approached the wash.

The three men were indeed gone. Fargo was set to turn around when a shadowy shape lying in low grass caught his eye. Pistol out, he investigated and learned that only two of the hardcases were still alive.

String Bean had taken a .52-caliber slug high in the chest, above the heart. The entry wound was no bigger than a large coin; the exit wound was the size of a man's fist. His eyes gaped blankly, and his mouth hung wide. Once the rain stopped, the buzzards would feast royally.

Fargo noted that the man had been stripped of everything of value. Gunbelt, revolver, bandanna, even String Bean's boots were gone, his pockets inside out.

Riding to the trail, Fargo sought tracks. Smudged prints revealed that three horses had headed northeast, toward Guthrie. At last he could relax. Jeb and the other one had given up and gone home.

The rain finally ended during the ride back to the wagon. Fargo heard shouts when still some distance off and brought the Ovaro to a gallop, fearing the worst. A single word was being yelled, over and over. When he was near enough, he realized they were calling his name.

Phinneas and his daughters hurried to meet him. "You had us worried," the father declared. "We were afraid you'd gone off and deserted us."

"*They* were worried," Belle corrected. "I wasn't. I knew you weren't the type to leave two women at the mercy of the elements and God knows what else."

"Did you see those bad men?" Liberty asked.

Fargo explained about the dead one as he stripped off his saddle and saddle blanket. He deposited both under the wagon so they would air out overnight and be dry by morning.

"I say good riddance to rubbish," Phinneas sniffed. "Ordinarily, I'm not a bloodthirsty person, but after the pain they inflicted on me, I can't profess to being upset because one of them died. They got what they were asking for."

Liberty stared at the bedroll under Fargo's arm and said, "It will be dark soon. Where do you intend to sleep?"

"Out here will do," Fargo said.

"Nonsense." This from Phinneas. "The ground is too wet. And you're already drenched to the skin. You'd be uncomfortable all night long." His thumb jabbed at the wagon. "We'll be warm and toasty inside. I insist you sleep inside with us. We already have a space cleared off on the floor for you."

The notion appealed to Fargo, and he admitted as much. The space was at the back. He had to fold his bedroll in half so there would be room to reach the small stove. His Sharps went in the corner, his saddlebags beside his bedding.

Liberty busied herself preparing supper while her father and sister resumed cleaning the mess. Phinneas clucked over the spilled ingredients like an irate mother hen over her scattered brood.

Fargo pulled his spare buckskin shirt from a saddlebag, then stripped off the one he wore. As he lowered it, he found himself the center of female attention. The two women openly ogled his muscular frame, Liberty going so far as to stare at the bulge below his belt.

"If you need to change your britches, we can step outside," Belle offered.

"I'm not the shy type," Fargo said. "But if it will make you feel any better, turn around until I'm done." Each faced the front, and he quickly stripped off his wet pants, dried his legs on his blanket, and squeezed into dry pants. When he looked up he almost laughed aloud; Liberty was peeking at him in a mirror.

24

Over the next hour Fargo gave the stallion a rubdown, un-hitched the team and staked the horses to picket pins, and examined the broken wheel. One spoke was cracked, the other split clean through, but there was nothing he could do until daylight.

Supper consisted of piping hot stew and delicious biscuits. Liberty hovered over Fargo, fulfilling his every whim, which, to his amusement, upset Belle. The sisters were in heated competition for his affection, unaware they were playing right into his hands.

During the meal Phinneas rambled on about the life of a patent medicine man. It was harder than most realized, he claimed. Drumming up business was half the trick, and to draw the crowds a man had to be part savvy showman and part miracle worker. "That's where my girls come in so handy," he said. "Without them I wouldn't make half the money I do."

"How so?" Fargo wondered.

Liberty piped up with, "Should we show him, Pa? Please, I'd love for him to see."

"Not now, sweetheart," Phinneas said, chuckling. "Save it for a surprise when we get to Rawbone."

"Let's hope there won't be any like those three from Guthrie this time around," Belle mentioned. "I swear. The next man who puts his grimy paws on me without my say-so is liable to eat his teeth."

"Now, now. That's no way to talk." Phinneas dipped his spoon into his bowl. "I admit you must tolerate more than your share of riffraff, but that's part of the life we've chosen for ourselves. And you know in your hearts I'd never let you come to any harm."

"You can't be watching over us every minute of every day," Belle said. "One of these times we'll be jumped, and there won't be someone as nice as Fargo around to pull our fat out of the fire."

"Are you implying that I'm too old to take care of my own? That I should quit?"

"No," Belle said wearily, as if they had discussed the same thing many times previously with the same result. "We'll stand by you through thick and thin, come what may."

In honor of the special occasion Liberty had baked four fruit tarts, the pie crust filled with peaches from a tin can. As Fargo was forking some into his mouth, she inquired, "Do you like it?"

"The best I've ever had," Fargo flattered her.

Liberty gave her sister a smug look of triumph. "I'm the cook in our family," she boasted. "Belle can't boil water without burning the pot."

"At least I can shoot something to put *in* the pot," the brunette countered. "We'd all starve if we had to rely on you for our meals."

"Men like to do their own hunting," Liberty said. "All they're interested in is someone who can fix tasty meals."

"Not all men are so narrow-minded." Belle refused to admit defeat. She glanced at Fargo. "Are they, Skye?"

Phinneas came to the rescue before Fargo could answer. "Enough, girls. We didn't invite him to join us to pester him to death. Allow him to finish his meal in peace."

Afterward, Fargo ventured outdoors to check on the Ovaro. The storm had long since sped eastward, and a multitude of stars sparkled in the firmament. As he stood leaning against the wagon, listening to the rattle of pots and pans inside, someone slipped noiselessly over the side.

"Mind company?" Belle asked.

"Shouldn't you be helping your sister do the dishes?" Fargo teased.

"We take turns." Belle planted her feet in front of him, her hands on her hips, her shoulders thrust back so her breasts strained against her dress. "Lucky me."

"Isn't your father still awake?"

"Yes. But he's too busy sorting to pay any attention to us."

"I'd rather wait until he's asleep."

"Not scared, are you?" Belle taunted.

In response Fargo looped his left arm around her back and pulled her full form flush against him. His right hand swooped to her breast as he mashed his lips onto hers. She gasped lightly, then melted into him, her mouth trembling, her chest heaving, her pelvis grinding into his groin. Automatically his manhood surged.

Out on the plain crickets chirped and somewhere an owl hooted, sounds that assured Fargo the night was tranquil, and he could concentrate on the matter at hand. His fingers kneaded the soft flesh on her yielding buttocks and dove between her legs from the rear.

Belle arched her spine and tried to suck his tongue down her throat. Tentatively her right hand crept down his body to his throbbing pole and stroked it.

Fargo shifted, pinning her against the wagon, freeing both hands to cup her globes and squeeze while his knee rubbed her nether mound. She panted in his ear, "Oh, God!" and dug her long fingernails into his broad shoulders. "What you do to me!"

The feeling was mutual, but Fargo was too busy licking her neck and throat to bother answering. He unfastened the top button, then the next, exposing part of her breast. Bending his elbow, he plunged his left hand under the material and located her hard nipple. A tweak brought a violent shudder. Deftly, he worked the breast free and sucked greedily.

"Ohhhh . . . ," Belle began, then caught herself, stifling her moan. She tensed, breaking contact to listen. The rasp of the door opening made her shove Fargo from her, fingers flying as she smoothed her clothes and composed herself.

Fargo, expecting her father, stepped between her and the front of the wagon to screen her from view. But it was a blond head that poked out and a bubbly voice that greeted him.

"Here you are! I just got done with the dishes and was hoping I'd have you all to myself." Liberty bounded from the seat and clasped his callused hands in hers. "Did you just hear a coyote?"

"No."

"Thought I did. But no matter. What would you say to a moonlit stroll?"

"Can I tag along?" Belle said mischievously, stepping around him.

"Where did you come from?" Liberty demanded in a huff.

"I've been here all the time. Fargo and I are having a pleasant talk. So why don't you prove you have good manners and leave us alone?"

"I have as much right to his company as you do," Liberty stated.

"Is that a fact?"

Fargo shut their petty bickering from his mind and hunkered

down to idly pluck at the grass. It had been a long day, and he was ready for a good night's sleep. Suddenly he became aware the crickets were silent. And the Ovaro had stopped grazing to gaze off into the darkness, its nostrils flaring. Instantly, Fargo whirled, seized the two women, and yanked them down next to him.

"What the devil?" Liberty blurted.

"Quiet!" Fargo commanded gruffly. "There's something out there."

"What?" Belle whispered.

Fargo used his ears and nose in an attempt to find out. He still heard nothing, an ominous sign. Since Comanches sometimes raided in the region, and the Kiowa-Apaches had been kicking up their heels of late, there was the possibility of a war party being abroad. Often they gave themselves away by the telltale pungent scent of bear fat, a principal ingredient in the sticky salve warriors used to stiffen their hair to the consistency of iron. But he smelled only dank earth and the horses.

Wild beasts were the second possibility. Fargo searched the area in front of the wagon where the lantern glow radiating through the doorway spread for a dozen yards, but he did not see a single set of blazing eyes.

A metallic click issued from the gloom.

"Phinneas, get down!" Fargo shouted, shoving the sisters flat as the night spat flame and lead. Slugs ripped into the wagon, sending chips of wood sailing.

Fargo counted the two gun flashes as his Colt cleared leather. He aimed at the sparks of light, banging off two shots at each. The unseen assassins directed their rifle fire at him instead, bullets thudding into the panels on either side, compelling him to flatten or become a human sieve.

Rolling to the right, Fargo adopted a two-handed grip and aimed at the nearest gun flash. He fired once, eliciting a screech of torment. A muffled cry rang out, then the pounding of heavy footsteps as the assassins fled.

Not about to let them escape, Fargo took several long strides and vaulted onto the stallion. Bareback, holding the pinto's mane, he galloped in the direction he thought the pair were taking. Hoofbeats confirmed he had pegged their position, and he gave the Ovaro its head, but no sooner had he done so than the pinto squealed and tumbled into a headlong fall that pitched Skye Fargo face first toward the ground.

3

A city-bred man would have died then and there, his neck snapped like a dry twig or his spine crumpled like a disjointed chain.

But Fargo's reflexes were the reflexes of a cougar, of a man who had spent his entire life on the raw frontier where speed and agility often meant the difference between living and dying. As he shot earthward, he tucked his chin to his chest and hunched his shoulders to absorb the bruising impact that jarred every bone in his body. He rolled as he hit, his momentum propelling him for eight or nine yards, and came to rest on his back, dazed but otherwise unscathed.

Fargo's first thought was for the Ovaro. Shoving upright, he moved unsteadily toward the stallion, which was struggling to stand. He didn't recall a gun flash at the moment they fell so he knew the pinto hadn't been shot. Something, though, had brought it crashing down, perhaps a prairie dog hole, and gnawing dread filled his head with a mental image of a shattered leg and the unsavory task he would have to perform if that was the case.

The Ovaro gained its feet, the pumping of its lungs like the pumping of a bellows. Badly frightened by the spill, as any horse would be, it shook from head to tail.

Fargo patted the pinto's neck, said, "There, there, boy," and squatted to run his hands over each front leg. Neither had been injured. He did the same with the rear legs and grinned in relief on finding them undamaged. Stroking the stallion, he calmed it, then mounted.

The assassins were long gone, leaving a mystery in their wake. Who had they been? Fargo mused as he headed back. Indians would sneak right up to the wagon and do the job silently, using tomahawks, knives, or war clubs. Outlaws wouldn't bother wasting their ammo unless certain the loot was worth the risk. No, a hunch told him that he owed Jeb and the other hardcase for nearly losing the pinto, and he would pay them back in kind when the opportunity presented itself.

Belle and Liberty were out from under the wagon, Belle ready with her rifle. Phinneas was outside, too, as pale as a sheet. "Did they get away?" he asked nervously.

"Afraid so," Fargo said, sliding off.

"Did you get a good look at the varmints?" Liberty wanted to know. "Did you see who they were?"

"No."

"I'll bet I know," Belle said. "It's those two sons of bitches from earlier today. They want revenge, and they're going to hound us all the way to Rawbone to get it."

Phinneas gnawed on his lower lip. "Do you think they'll try again tonight?"

"There's no telling," Fargo said, "so I'll stay out here until morning." No one objected. He went inside, brought out his bedroll and belongings. Rather than sleep in the open, he made room under the wagon. Then he moved the horses closer. Satisfied, he lay on his stomach, the Sharps at his side, and listened to Boggs and the women moving about above him.

Sleep was a long time coming. Fargo dozed fitfully, awakening at the faintest noise. Coyotes yipped occasionally, and once the plaintive wail of a lonesome wolf wafted on the breeze. The whole time the crickets kept up their steady serenade.

It was the scrape of a shoe on wood that snapped Fargo fully awake. A pair of slim legs moved stealthily past the broken wheel and paused, the feet twisting around as the person shifted to look behind.

Fargo rose on an elbow, making a bet with himself as to which one it would be. The swirl of dark hair when she bent down confirmed it, and then Belle was lying in front of him, a sheer satiny robe draped carelessly around her lush body, her lipid eyes pools of smoldering desire.

"I couldn't sleep," she whispered.

"Imagine that." Fargo couldn't resist baiting her.

"I figured you might like to take up where we left off when Liberty interrupted us."

"Are you sure she won't again?"

Belle shook her head. "Not a chance. I made certain they were both in dreamland before I came out." She wriggled nearer. The tip of her nose was a fraction of an inch from his. "I can't seem to get you out of my mind no matter how hard I try."

"We'll be parting company at Rawbone," Fargo reminded her.

"I know. Don't get me wrong. I'm not looking to get hitched." Belle rested a warm hand on his neck and puckered her rosy lips. "It's just that you have an air about you, a knack for making a woman's insides as hot as a tin roof on a scorching summer's day."

"Do I?" Fargo smirked, pulling her to him. "This I'll have to see for myself." Without warning he plunged his right hand under the lower folds of her robe. She involuntarily stiffened as his fingers kneaded her smooth flesh. Her lips parted to receive his, and she glued herself to him, a fluttering moan issuing from low in her throat.

Fargo lowered her flat onto her back. His chest cushioned by her large breasts, he nibbled on her ears while his hand gently eased her legs wide. The heat she gave off was incredible. He ran a finger around the rim of her womanhood, then slowly inserted it, feeling her quiver under him.

"I want you so much," Belle husked softly.

Kneeling between her bent knees, Fargo undid the robe, his pole tingling at the sight of the treasures revealed. He took a nipple into his mouth and twirled it with his tongue. She snaked fingers into his hair, pressed hard. Simultaneously, her hips thrust upward, driving into him with a rhythmic slap again and again. An urgency drove her movements, a craving akin to that of a person parched with thirst who was handed a full water skin.

"What's your rush?" Fargo rose up long enough to ask her. She grasped his head, guiding him to her stomach. He licked her navel, her flat tummy, the rounded tops of her thighs. A tantalizing aroma lured him lower, and when his mouth closed on her pleasure knob, she raked him with her nails, drawing blood.

Fargo stuck his tongue into her slick tunnel, flicking back and forth. The sensation drove her wild with passion. Willowy legs waving crazily, she rotated her hips to heighten the exquisite sensation. He had to grab her bottom and hold her down in order to keep from being bucked aside.

Belle huffed and puffed and mewed as Fargo drove her to the brink of release. And beyond. Without warning she began to cry out, but suppressed her wanton shriek at the first syllable. Her body erupted in an orgy of convulsions that seemed to go on forever.

Fargo could do little more than hang on and keep licking. He tasted her womanly nectar as she gushed over his chin. Belle released him and writhed uncontrollably, lost in sexual delirium. For minutes this lasted. Then, abruptly, she subsided, going limp, her arms falling at her side, her legs swinging outward. She was totally spent.

But Fargo was just getting warmed up. He gave her gorgeous breasts more attention while she lay with closed eyes, lost in a blissful rapture. Her lips reacted weakly to his kisses. It took the sudden thrust of his organ into her innermost recesses to jerk her from her lethargy.

"Oh my God!" Belle said. She clamped her arms and legs to him and gazed with wonder at his face. "I don't know if I can take any more."

"Let's find out," Fargo said.

Mouths and hips fused, they coupled at a leisurely pace, Fargo unwilling to rush. He stroked with the practiced skill of long experience, intent on pleasing her as much as he pleased himself. There was barely enough room under the wagon for him to prop himself on his arms, but he managed.

The whole time Fargo monitored the crickets and other night sounds. He'd been caught napping once. He wasn't going to make the same mistake twice.

However many lovers Belle had known, she evidently had never known one to last so long. Her amazement grew, as did her ecstasy. Over and over she cooed, "Oh! Oh! Oh!" adding now and then, "Never like this!" or "You're the best, the very best!"

Unexpectedly, Fargo felt a cool, moist object brush his shoulder blade. Puzzled, he glanced up and saw the Ovaro. Their frantic movements had carried them partly out from under the wagon. He swatted at the pinto muzzle, but the puckish stallion stayed where it was, watching.

Belle never noticed. She was lost to the world, lost to herself, lost to him. Eyes hooded, lips glistening, her body sheathed in sweat, she made love with an abandon born of long abstinence. Having crested once, she took longer this time.

Fargo held himself in until pulsations deep within her alerted him to her impending climax. Then he pumped with fury, familiar constrictions in his throat and his groin signaling his release. He exploded, pinpoints of bright light wheeling before him, and she did likewise. In unison they gained the pinnacle, in unison they coasted down from the summit and were still in each other's arms.

After a while the cool air revitalized Fargo enough for him to slide off the brunette. He draped a forearm on his forehead and absently stared at the stars. A shadow passed over them, blotting a handful out. Then the Ovaro's muzzle descended, pressing full on his mouth. "Damn you," he growled, pushing hard. "Your breath stinks to high heaven."

"What?" Belle practically yelled, coming up off the bedroll so fast she cracked her skull on the wagon. Indignant, she slapped him on the arm. "I'll have you know I gargle with salt water daily!"

"I didn't mean you—," Fargo said, but got no further. A loud thump overhead interrupted him, and Phinneas called out.

"Belle? Belle? Was that you? Where are you?"

"What the dickens is all the commotion about?" Liberty threw in sleepily.

"Oh Lord!" Belle whispered. Frantically scampering into the open, she fumbled with her robe and darted forward.

Fargo hauled on his pants. It wouldn't do for Phinneas to catch him indecent. The wagon creaked as Belle climbed up, and he heard her footsteps on the floorboards.

"Where have you been?" her father asked curtly.

"I heard a noise and went out to see what it was," Belle glibly replied.

"In your robe?" Phinneas said suspiciously.

"Should I have traipsed outside naked?"

"No, no. Certainly not." There was a pause. "Did Fargo hear the noise?"

"It was one of the horses."

"That's all? Thank goodness." Phinneas coughed. "I'll be

34

glad when we reach Rawbone and put this nightmare behind us."

"You're not the only one," Liberty said.

More was said, but in voices so low Fargo couldn't distinguish the words. Not thinking anything of it, he eased onto his side and placed the Sharps alongside him. Dawn was still hours off, and he needed a few hours sleep so he closed his eyes and let his fatigue overwhelm him.

Mere minutes seemed to go by, but in reality it was two hours later when the Ovaro snorted, rousing Fargo to face the predawn chill. Rifle in hand, he stood and studied the landscape. To the south appeared the reason for the snort, a large lumbering black bear ambling westward. It showed no interest in the wagon or the stock. Full from a long night of grubbing for anything edible, it headed for its den.

Fargo stretched and made a circuit of the area. A faint pink tinge streaked the eastern horizon. To the north a small herd of antelope browsed. He would have shot one except the Boggs's were still asleep.

That changed shortly after a glorious sunrise. Liberty was first up. She sat on the seat, combing her disheveled golden hair. "Good morning, Skye."

Fargo grunted.

"Did you sleep well? I seem to recollect a commotion of some sort in the middle of the night." Deviltry animated her features. "Wasn't my sister out here without hardly any clothes on?"

"I didn't notice."

"That will be the day." Liberty laughed. "You're like a hawk, Skye Fargo. You don't miss a thing."

"If you say so."

Her failure to provoke him provoked her. "I must admit I'm disappointed you didn't take an interest in me first. Now you'll never know what you missed out on."

Fargo, to hide his grin, stepped to the Ovaro and scratched behind its ears.

"Didn't you hear me?" Liberty asked.

"I heard you."

"Well?"

"Well what?"

"Aren't you the least bit upset?"

"Why should I be?"

Liberty shook her brush at him. "Men! You're all alike. There isn't one of you who can see the forest for the trees."

"You've lost me," Fargo said innocently.

So angry her cheeks were scarlet, Liberty stormed into the wagon and slammed the door. Something crashed to the floor and Phinneas yelped.

Fargo let the horses free to graze, then busied himself rolling up and tying his bedroll and cleaning the Sharps. He had just finished when the patent medicine man climbed stiffly down, flanked by the two lovelies. Belle gave him a smile that would melt sugar. Liberty gave him the sort of look that would curdle milk.

"Ready to fix the wheel?" Phinneas inquired.

"Do you have spare spokes?" Fargo rejoined. "If not, you won't be going anywhere any time soon. There isn't a tree within twenty miles of here."

Phinneas hooked his thumbs in his vest. "Mr. Fargo, you underestimate me. I told you that I've spent most of my life in this trade. I've lost track of the number of wheels I've had to fix over the years. Most definitely I have everything we need."

And he did. In a box attached to the back were a half dozen spokes. More crucial was the jack. Made of heavy iron-bound wood, it could lift the heaviest wagons on the market. Fargo set it under the axle and turned the hand crank that worked the rack-and-pinion gears. When the wheel was high enough, Phinneas set the pawl that kept the jack from slipping.

The better part of the morning was spent in removing the wheel, prying open the rim, and aligning the new spokes in their proper sockets. Fargo did the most of the work. He didn't mind since he figured he owed the Boggs for their hospitality.

The temperature had climbed into the upper eighties before Fargo was done. Moping his brow, he stepped back and regarded his handiwork with approval. It was rare that he got to work with tools, and he liked it.

Belle brought him a glass of water. "Nice job. You have talents I never imagined."

"I've scouted for a few wagon trains," Fargo disclosed. "Whenever a wagon breaks down in hostile Indian country, everyone who can helps out."

"Speaking of Indians," Phinneas said from the shady spot

where he had collapsed an hour ago, "is there any truth to the rumor of a Comanche war party being seen in this territory within the past few weeks?"

"First I've heard of it."

"The story goes that a homestead to the east was attacked and burned, the settler and his family butchered." Phinneas frowned. "I would hate to run into the savages responsible. They'd show my girls no mercy."

Or sell them to slavers, Fargo thought, but kept it to himself. "Let's hit the trail," he advised. "It'll take us four days to reach Rawbone even if we push."

Rounding up the team took longer than Fargo counted on. One of Boggs's horses evidently figured it deserved the day off and trotted off whenever Fargo approached. Exasperated, he saddled the Ovaro and lassoed the stubborn mare. Once she was in harness, she calmed down.

By noon they had covered only a few miles. Belle drove while her father and Liberty continued sorting the mess inside. Phinneas insisted on having everything in order by the time they reached Rawbone.

Fargo rode beside the team and listened to Belle relate the story of her early years. Life had been hard in one respect, with the family always on the go. The sisters had missed not having a permanent home, and had made few lasting friendships. On the other hand, they'd enjoyed traveling and getting to meet new people. So it all balanced out in the end.

Evening found them camped in a hollow. Fargo slept out under the wagon again, hoping one of the women would pay him a visit. Neither did.

The next day was more of the same, and the next. Gradually the country changed. The prairie gave way to rolling hills dotted with trees. By the afternoon of the third day tracts of lush woodland broke the monotony of the grassland.

That evening Fargo located a small winding stream and chose an adjacent clearing for their camp site. Instead of eating in the wagon as was their habit, Fargo made a fire outside and Liberty prepared rabbit stew from two rabbits Fargo shot. The night was crystal clear, the air crisp, the meal delicious. Fargo sat on a log set near the crackling flames and ate until his belly was fit to burst.

"Tomorrow afternoon we should reach Rawbone," Phinneas commented.

"I can hardly wait, Pa," Liberty said. "I need to buy a new dress and some cosmetic cream."

Her father snorted. "A pretty girl like you, with your creamy complexion? That stuff is a waste of money if you ask me."

"How do you think I keep my complexion so smooth?" Liberty argued. "All this heat and wind doesn't do it any good. A woman has to work awful hard nowadays to keep herself in shape." She sighed, then glared at Fargo. "And for what? You'd think more men would have taken notice of me by now. At the rate I'm going, I'll wind up an old maid with no husband and no grandchildren to sit on my knee."

"I wouldn't worry," Phinneas assured her. "Sooner or later the right man will come along. For both of you."

"So you've been saying for the past three years," Liberty said. "One hasn't come along yet."

"There have been a few gentlemen interested in you," Phinneas said.

"A dirt farmer. A store clerk. A livery owner. Some prospects!" Liberty shook her head sadly. "No, I'll end my days a spinster. I just know it."

Fargo saw her peek at him out of one corner of her eye, but he made no comment. Long ago he'd learned to avoid taking the bait when a woman was on a fishing expedition.

Belle rested her bowl on her legs and said, "You have no one to blame but yourself, Sis. You would have been hitched long ago if you weren't so finicky."

"Me?"

"That store clerk in Wyandotte was decent enough, and he fell for you hard. But you wouldn't have him because of a few measly warts."

"There were more than a few," Liberty said. "He had six or seven big ones." She shuddered and grimaced. "I couldn't bear to think of those things touching me. Ugh!"

Fargo threw back his head and roared. He received a withering glare as Liberty rose, walked over to take his empty bowl, and flounced into the wagon.

"Pay her no mind, Mr. Fargo," Phinneas said. "I'm afraid I

spoiled her a tad when she was little and now she's a regular fussbudget."

"Tell the truth, Pa," Belle chided. "Liberty is worse than fussy. She's a royal pain in the—"

"Belle! Behave! Ladies don't use that kind of language."

"Oh, Pa."

Chuckling, Fargo stood and went to fetch his bedroll and saddle, stacked at the rear of the wagon. He planned to turn in early and get an early start. The sooner Boggs and the girls were safely in town, the sooner he could resume his delayed journey to Texas.

Fargo bent to grip the saddle horn and was straightening when he saw the three tethered horses all staring into the trees. In light of everything that had happened, he was taking no chances. Depositing the saddle, he moved to the edge of the clearing.

Deep in the woods an irate squirrel chattered. A few cicadas were singing. Nothing else made noise, nor did Fargo see anything move. The horses still stared, the team animals fidgeting restlessly.

"Is something wrong?" Phinneas called.

"I don't know," Fargo admitted. He walked several feet to the left, wishing he'd brought a torch. Suddenly a soft rustling in leafy bushes caused the horses to whinny and stamp. Crouching, Fargo raked the thin branches from top to bottom without spotting whatever was out there.

Deciding to fetch a firebrand, Fargo pivoted on a boot heel and strode toward the fire. He saw Belle looking right at him, saw her eyes widen in startled terror an instant before a heavy form slammed into his back, knocking him to his hands and knees. Fargo began to rise, spinning as he did, his hand falling to his Colt. He had no idea what had attacked him, but he certainly didn't suspect the creature confronting him.

It was a wolf.

4

Wolves rarely attacked people. Like most animals they fled at the sight or scent of humans. But also like most animals, there were exceptions to the rule. Starving wolves wouldn't hesitate to stalk a grown man. And many an old-timer claimed that on special nights of the year wolves were overcome by blood lust and went on killing sprees that left scores of deer, sheep, or cattle dead.

Fargo had never placed much stock in superstition. So on setting eyes on the wolf, he sought a logical explanation for its assault and found it. Weeks ago the wolf's left rear leg had been sheared off at the hock, perhaps by the fanged teeth of a steel trap. The wound had healed over, but unable to hunt effectively, the wolf had been reduced to skin and bones. Desperate for food, it had ignored its instinctive fear and stalked the tied horses.

Now, as Fargo drew his pistol, the wolf snarled and lunged, unpredictably fast on short spurts despite the loss of one foot. Fargo cleared leather, but had to release the Colt to grasp hold of the wolf's throat with both hands as the beast plowed into him. The impact bowled him over. He heard a scream. He heard the wolf's slavering jaws snap shut inches from his neck. Heaving with all his might, he flung the wolf from him and shoved erect.

Or tried to. The wolf was on him before he could unwind, and again Fargo went down under the feral onslaught, the glistening jaws missing his exposed jugular by a hair. Fargo rolled and pushed, but the wolf only slid a few inches, then tried to bite off his hands. Warm breath fanned his fingers and drops of saliva dotted his palm.

Scuttling backward, Fargo gained one knee and braced for another charge. He twisted as the wolf leaped, and the predator missed and went sailing past. Whirling, Fargo swept his hand under his right boot, freeing his Arkansas toothpick. He held the knife low and got his left forearm up to protect his face as the wolf came at him yet one more time.

The wolf yipped when the blade sank to the hilt. Wrenching sideways, it scurried in a tight circle, seeking an opening.

Fargo circled too, the bloody toothpick close to his leg. His next stroke would be a killing stroke, and he tensed for the spring.

A rifle blasted, the slug smacking into the ground in front of the wolf's nose. The ragged beast tried to flee, to spin, but in its haste was unable to retain its balance and toppled. A second shot struck it high on the rump. Yowling, the wolf planted both front feet and was rising when the Arkansas toothpick impaled it squarely in the chest.

Years of practice had gone into that throw. Fargo had aimed for the heart, and his aim had been unerring. He caught his breath while the wolf thrashed and growled, its actions growing weaker and weaker until at length it sagged, tongue lolling.

Belle materialized next to Fargo, smoke curling from the barrel of her rifle. "Sorry I missed the first time. I aimed low so I wouldn't accidentally wing you."

"You did fine." Fargo jerked out the toothpick, then wiped the blade on the wolf's fur.

Phinneas and Liberty walked up, both clearly shaken. "Are you all right?" the former asked.

Fargo nodded.

"That bite must sting," Liberty said, gingerly touching his back. "I'll tend it for you." Her dress swirled as she dashed off.

Craning his neck around, Fargo was surprised to discover the wolf had bitten him when it rammed into his back. He hadn't felt a thing, yet his buckskin shirt had a three-inch tear, and he'd suffered a gash almost as long.

"Do you think it's rabid?" Phinneas queried.

The idea shocked Fargo. Hunkering down, he examined the animal, but found none of the typical symptoms of rabies. "It's not," he said softly, gratefully. He'd seen a man die of rabies once and could not bear to think of undergoing a similar excruciating ordeal. No one should have to die like that.

Liberty returned, bearing one of her father's ointments.

"I'll do it," Belle volunteered, reaching for the jar.

"Not on your life," Liberty said, taking Fargo by the arm and leading him over to the log. In no-nonsense fashion she helped him remove his shirt and had him bend forward. She wiped the blood off with a clean, moist cloth, her fingers gentle, her manner considerate.

"I figured you'd be happy to see me bitten," Fargo remarked as she opened the jar. "You've been mad at me for days."

Liberty answered in a low tone so no one else could hear. "Silly man. You don't know diddly about women or you'd know how fond we are of stringing a handsome man like you along just for the thrill of it. I wasn't really mad. I was pretending."

"You could have fooled me," Fargo lied, his grin well hidden.

"I was jealous some, is all," Liberty went on as she dabbed the ointment on the wound. "Most men take an interest in me first and only spend the time of day with Belle if I don't show any interest." She dabbed harder, making him wince. "But not you. Belle batted those long eyelashes of hers, and you fell all over her like an elk in rut." She dabbed even harder. "Me, you ignored. Why? Don't you like blondes?"

Fargo grit his teeth as she poked him a third time. Grunting, he swiveled and took the jar. "I'll live longer if I do the rest myself."

"Sorry. I didn't mean to hurt you." Liberty sidled nearer. "But I must know. Why don't you think I'm attractive?"

"I do." Fargo sniffed the ointment, a green salve unlike any he'd ever come across. The odor was terrible, sort of like buffalo sweat, cow piss, and bear droppings all combined.

"Then why haven't you shown it?"

Fargo shrugged and promptly regretted it when the gash flooded with pain. "You've made it plan you're looking for someone to marry, and I'm not the marrying kind."

"That's the only reason?"

"I need another?"

"No," Liberty said, lightly running a finger across the muscles lining his shoulders. "But haven't you ever noticed that when a woman goes shopping for a new dress she likes to try on six or seven before she picks the one she wants?" Lowering her rosy lips to his ear, she whispered, "Tonight has to be the night. I'll try to sneak out after Pa falls asleep."

Fargo watched her pert fanny sashay around the fire, marveling at the outworking of fate. He had about given up on the notion of sharing a blanket with her, and now look at what had happened!

"What were the two of you talking about?" Belle asked. She had come up on him silently, carrying her rifle in the crook of her elbow. Distrust hardened her face and her voice.

"Nothing much," Fargo said. To divert her train of thought, he attempted to apply more ointment, but he couldn't bend his arm far enough. "Care to lend a hand?"

Without responding Belle took the jar and the cloth. Phinneas straggled to the log, brushing his hands on his pants. "I dragged the mangy carcass into the woods. The scent was upsetting the horses." He contemplated the trees. "Do you think the wolf was part of a pack?"

"I doubt it," Fargo said. "He couldn't keep up in his condition. My guess is that he was a *lobo*, fending for himself."

"I hope so," Phinneas said. He rubbed his hands as if he were cold. "This incident has been most unsettling. I doubt I'll be able to sleep a wink."

Apparently such was the case, because although Fargo stayed awake late, waiting for Liberty to show, she never did. The next morning, as he harnessed the team, she passed him on her way back from the stream and slowed long enough to whisper, "I want you to know that I had every intention of sneaking out last night, but Pa tossed and turned something terrible and woke up every so often. I dared not try."

"Just our luck," Fargo said.

"Are you planning to stay in Rawbone very long?" Liberty inquired hopefully. "We might be able to get together."

"I leave for Texas tomorrow morning," Fargo revealed. "I have some hard riding to do if I'm to get there on time."

"Oh well," Liberty said wistfully. "I reckon it's not meant to be."

Phinneas Boggs was more cheerful this day than Fargo had ever seen him. The patent medicine man handled the reins himself, urging the team to greater speed in his zeal to reach town. Toward the middle of the afternoon they came on a rickety sign bearing faded black letters: RAWBONE. POPULATION 71.

"At last!" Phinneas exclaimed, stopping. "Girls, it's time to prepare yourselves. We wouldn't want to disappoint our audience." To Fargo he said, "You're more than welcome to go the rest of the way with us, but there will be a short delay while my daughters get ready."

"Ready how?"

"You'll see," Phinneas said, his features like those of a gleeful chipmunk. "You'll see."

The wait was not very long. Both women, casting resigned looks at their father, went inside. Under five minutes later the door swung open, and Liberty slid out rather self-consciously and took her seat on the right side. Belle, showing a marked lack of enthusiasm, trailed her.

Fargo had been slouched over the saddle horn, his hat brim pulled low to ward off the blistering heat. On glancing up he gaped in amazement, then closed his mouth and drank in the female charms of the two sisters, saying, "There's more to this patent medicine business than I knew."

Liberty and Belle had exchanged their prim dresses for gaudy costumes the likes of which were only worn by dancers in saloon halls—except the dancers covered more of themselves. Liberty's outfit was a shocking red, Belle's a vivid blue, fitting so tightly their breasts bubbled at the top, on the verge of popping out if they breathed too hard. Bright white tassels hung from the sides and the front. Their legs were bare clear to their thighs; some might label the amount of skin exposed as downright sinful.

"Stick your tongue back in," Belle snapped.

Fargo started to reach for his mouth, caught himself, and laughed. "Can you blame me?" he challenged. "Go into town dressed like that and you're liable to cause a riot."

"Pa had this brainstorm, not us," Liberty said. "He needs to draw in crowds to hear his pitch and this does the trick."

"I bet it does," Fargo said dryly.

Phinneas chortled, happy his genius was appreciated. "When they were small I had them parade into each town ahead of the wagon, playing instruments. Liberty knows the flute, Belle the guitar. They would sing their little lungs out, and people would think they were so cute and gather to hear them. And when the girls were done singing, I would make my pitch." He fondly patted Belle's knee. "But as they grew older, not as many people came to listen. I needed a new lure, and one day after my dear wife passed on, I was in a dance hall and an inspiration came to me."

"It works like a charm, too," Liberty boasted. "Men flock around from all over once the word spreads."

"You'll see for yourself shortly," Phinneas promised.

The dusty ribbon that served as a road wound into the east end of Rawbone and out the west. A dozen drab, shoddy buildings lined its fringe. Two side streets sported a few frame houses and other establishments. And way off by itself to the south rose a fine three-story house as grand as the manor house of a feudal lord. Cattle grazed in a pasture beside it.

"Soon we'll have the money for that new dress you want," Phinneas assured Liberty, halting once more fifty yards out. "Let's get cracking."

Belle disappeared within and stepped out holding a guitar and a poster. The sisters climbed down, Liberty took the poster, and they strolled toward Rawbone side by side. While Belle strummed the guitar, tuning it, Phinneas goaded the team into a slow walk.

Fargo drifted to one side. He read the poster, which boldly advertised the arrival of the greatest patent medicine man in the history of western civilization and claimed cures for every ailment under the sun. "You go a bit overboard, don't you think?"

"Not at all," Phinneas disagreed. "The public is fickle, sir. Every true salesman knows that the only way to get the attention of the average nincompoop is to pound him or her over the head with a hammer. Or its equivalent." He nodded at the poster Liberty held aloft. "I've exaggerated somewhat, yes. But only to heighten interest in my remedies. No one has ever held it against me."

"Yet," Fargo said.

Few citizens were abroad in the heat of the day. Those who were saw the small procession and turned. On cue Belle played with gusto, singing in a strong warble, "Now we gather at the river, the . . ."

It was too ridiculous for words. Fargo shook his head and

chuckled, veering to the left to a hitching post in front of a general store.

A burly man wearing an apron came out, two elderly ladies in tow. "What on earth is going on, Mr. Richards?" asked one.

"Why, it's a medicine show, Mrs. Peachtree," Richards replied in disbelief. "Ain't seen one of them in nigh on ten years."

"It's disgusting, I say," declared the second lady. "Look at how those hussies are dressed! Why, I wore more when I came into this vale of tears."

"The poor dears will suffer heatstroke," Mrs. Peachtree commented.

"It would serve them right," her irritated friend responded.

Richards, wiping his thick hands on his apron, looked at Fargo. "Are you with them, mister?"

"You might say that," Fargo allowed. Sliding down, he wound the reins around the post and brushed some of the dust from his buckskins.

"I hope for your sake they're not a confidence troupe," Richards said. "The folks hereabouts wouldn't take kindly to being swindled."

"They're as honest as they come," Fargo said. More and more people appeared, from every single building in sight. A rowdy bunch pushed through the bat-wing doors of a saloon across the street and started whistling and making catcalls at the sisters.

"Uh-oh," Mrs Peachtree said. "The Holman boys are in town. There could be trouble."

"Who are they?" Fargo questioned.

"You've never heard of Cull Holman?" Mrs. Peachtree said. "Goodness. He's only the biggest man in these parts." She pointed a bony finger southward at the distant roof of the huge house, visible above the saloon. "That's his place, mister. His two boys are as ornery as they come, and the men who work for him aren't much better." She smacked her thin lips in disapproval. "If those young ladies are your friends, you'd best keep an eye on them."

"Thanks for the warning," Fargo said. By now the wagon was a third of the way into town and had stopped near the general store. Phinneas was unhinging the right side panel so he could display his wares while Liberty paraded in a circle wav-

46

ing the poster and Belle continued singing religious songs, of all things.

From all directions flocked Rawbone's residents, men, women, and children, forming around the front of the wagon.

Fargo strolled toward the saloon. The Holman outfit was drifting down the street, mingling with everyone else. He strode into the cool interior to find no one there but the bald barkeep who was hurrying toward the entrance. "How about a drink before you go?"

The man paused, glancing at the doors. "I don't want to miss anything . . . ," he hedged.

"A glass of whiskey to wash down the dust is all I need," Fargo said.

"Oh, hell," the bartender said. Stepping around the counter, he poured quickly. "You can pay me when I get back," he said and breezed by.

Fargo carried the drink outside and leaned against a corner post. He sipped, grunting as the coffin varnish burned a path down his throat and into his gut. His whole body trembled, and he slapped his thigh. "Damn. Good red-eye," he remarked aloud.

"Gordon never waters his booze down like some do," said a deep voice to his rear.

The speaker was a tall man, graying at the temples, his expression kindly but firm, a battered tin star pinned to his vest.

"Didn't figure this town big enough for a lawdog," Fargo said.

"Cull Holman wanted one, and what Cull Holman wants, Cull Holman gets," the marshal said. "My handle is Erskine. Worked as a law officer down in New Orleans before I got hired for this job." His green eyes narrowed. "Don't I know you from somewhere?"

"Could be," Fargo said. "I get around." He swallowed more whiskey, aware of being studied from hat to spurs.

"I saw you ride in with the medicine show," Erskine mentioned. "But you don't strike me as being a patent medicine man. What's your connection with them?"

Fargo lowered his drink and transferred the glass to his left hand, freeing his right so he could drape his palm over the butt of his Colt. "That's my business. And I don't like having someone pry into my personal affairs."

"Sheath your claws, *hombre*," Erskine said. "I'm just doing my job. For all I know that Boggs feller is a swindler and you're in cahoots with him."

"We met on the trail, is all," Fargo revealed. "Some gents from Guthrie were giving Boggs and his girls a hard time, and I had to teach the varmints how to behave themselves."

"These men have names?"

"The only one I heard was Jeb."

"Jeb Baxter? You bucked him and lived?" Erskine cocked his head. "You must be tough as nails. Most who brace Jeb wind up as worm food."

"Have you seen him in the past few days?"

"No," Erskine said. "He passes through every now and then, but never steps too far out of line because he's not about to rile Cull Holman and Holman doesn't take kindly to rowdies. Unless they're *his* rowdies." The marshal faced the crowd and added, "I've heard tell Jeb is wanted over to Texas for rustling and robbery, but I've never seen a circular on him. Which is too bad. I'd love to throw him behind bars and lose the key."

"If he shows while I'm here, you won't need to bother."

The lawman digested the news, then sniffed. "Another thing Cull Holman isn't too fond of is gunplay."

Fargo downed the last of his drink. "Why do I get the impression this Holman runs things here?"

"Because he does," Erskine said. "Rawbone is his, lock, stock, and barrel. He was the first white man in this area. He mined some, brought in some cattle, carved himself a small empire in the middle of nowhere. Then he got tired of going all the way to Wyandotte all the time for his supplies and built himself his own town."

"I've always wanted my own town," Fargo quipped.

"It's not like you think. Holman is tough but fair. He lets everyone do as they please so long as they don't make trouble." Erskine glanced at him. "The key word is trouble. Make any and I'll have to come down on you, hard."

"Thanks for the warning."

Fargo had met individuals like Holman before, self-made men who set themselves up like kings, lording it over everyone in their domain. Fair or not, Holman didn't sound any different from the rest. Cross a man like him and you paid the price, which might be your life.

A loud bellow down the street drew Fargo's attention to the wagon where Phinneas Boggs had assembled dozens of jars and containers and stood with arms upraised.

"Ladies and gentlemen! Friends! Countrymen! I bid you greetings! I hope you've enjoyed the sterling entertainment provided by my lovely daughters. Now it's time to talk about the reason for our visit, about why I've gathered you here today." Phinneas was in his element. He stopped for dramatic effect, sweeping the crowd with a mesmerizing glance.

"I daresay there isn't one of you who hasn't been sick at one time or another," the patent medicine man resumed. "We all suffer the pangs of being mortal. Whether it's the common cold, gout, arthritis, or something else, we've all known misery. And when we're afflicted we all wish we could be well again.

"Like the Good Book says. There's a time to be born, and a time to die. A time to plant, and a time to pluck up that which is planted. A time to kill, and a time to heal.

"And this is where I come in, where my services can benefit each and every one of you. For what else is a man in my profession if not first and foremost a healer?"

The majority listened intently to the pitch. But there were five men, the Holman bunch, who had been pushing ever closer to the wagon as Boggs talked. At that moment, with Phinneas catching his breath, one of their number in a black hat walked up to the wagon, seized the front of Boggs's shirt, and roughly hauled him forward, knocking medicines right and left.

"So you're a healer, huh?" the man in the black hat said and shook Boggs violently. "I say we make you prove it."

blow to the man holding Belle, knocking the man onto his back in a cloud of dirt. Fargo remarked the one holding

5

Skye Fargo sprinted toward the crowd, knowing he would be too late. He saw the troublemaker raise a stony fist and saw Boggs flinch in anticipation of the blow. Some of the onlookers gasped, some gaped, but none made a move to interfere although a few looked as if they wanted to.

Then a feline fury with brunette hair hurtled out of nowhere and pounced on the young man in the black hat. Belle had dropped her guitar to attack the man like a woman possessed. Her nails raked his cheeks, leaving ten bleeding slash marks. Shocked by the onslaught, the man let go of Phinneas and tried to seize Belle, but she was too much for him to handle. Her knee rammed his crotch, doubling him over, and she was drawing back her fist to punch him full in the mouth when another of the Holman outfit recovered his wits sufficiently to leap to his partner's aid. The second man gripped Belle from behind, trying to pin her arms.

He might have succeeded, too, if not for a second shrieking whirlwind, a blond madwoman who flung herself at him with as much ferocity as that displayed by her sister. Liberty wasn't as strong or quick as Belle, but she was formidable in her own right. Her nails opened a wicked cut on the second man, from a corner of his eye to his chin.

All hell threatened to bust loose. The other Holman men jumped toward the sisters while some in the crowd screamed and several edged forward. The man in the black hat had touched his ravaged cheeks, glared at his blood smeared hands, and was reaching for his six-shooter.

It was then Fargo got there. He didn't waste words, demanding an explanation. He didn't try to calm everyone. He simply ran right up to the man in the black hat and flattened him with a solid right to the jaw. Pivoting, Fargo delivered a blow to the man holding Belle, knocking the man onto his backside. A swift shift, and Fargo punched the one holding Liberty.

Now there were four people on the ground. A woman in the crowd caterwauled hysterically. And the last two Holman men had swung toward Fargo and were about to go for their hardware.

Two booming shots froze everyone. Marshal Erskine strode into the middle of the melee, his revolver at waist level. "That will be enough!" he roared. "The next one who lifts a finger against someone else loses a hand."

No one was inclined to dispute him. Fargo kept his eyes on the men who worked for Holman as Belle and Liberty ran to their father and helped him up.

The man in the black hat rose on one knee, a hand rubbing his bruised jaw. "You saw!" he bellowed at the lawman. "This son of a bitch hit me!"

"I saw, Johnny," Erskine said.

"Then you know what to do, don't you?" the one named Johnny snapped. "I want him arrested so we can give him a fair trial and string him up from a cottonwood."

"I'm afraid not," the marshal said.

Johnny blinked, flushed with rage, and jabbed a thumb at Fargo. "Are you saying you're not going to arrest this saddle tramp? You're siding with him against *me*? Is that what you want me to tell my father."

"Tell him anything you like," Erskine said. "And while you're at it, tell Cull that you were the one who started this ruckus, that you were the one who picked on an old man and a couple of women. And be sure to tell him you'd been drinking heavily beforehand."

For a few seconds Fargo thought Johnny Holman was going to draw on the lawman. Holman's fingers twitched dangerously close to his pistol. Fargo was ready to add his gun to the marshal's should the others join in, but the younger Holman abruptly lowered both arms, cursed, and stormed off, his four men nipping at his heels like a pack of loyal hound dogs.

Fargo looked at the marshal with a new measure of respect. It had taken grit to stand up to the son of the most powerful man in the territory, grit to do what was right despite what might happen. He nodded at the departing figures. "Holman should keep his son on a short leash."

Erskine sighed. "Johnny is Cull's pride and joy. In his eyes the boy can do no wrong. Truth is, Johnny Holman is hell with the hide off." He glanced at the great house to the south. "By sundown I figure the old man himself will pay me a visit."

"But you were only doing your duty." This from Phinneas, who was straightening his vest and jacket.

"Maybe so," the marshal agreed, "but blood is thicker than water, as the old saw goes. Cull Holman won't take kindly to having his son shamed in public." He slid his pistol into his holster. "Mr. Boggs, you'd be wise to get on that wagon of yours and make yourself scarce."

Belle bristled. "Why should we run? We've done nothing wrong."

Liberty nodded. "And it's your job to see that no harm comes to our pa or ourselves."

"I can only do so much, ma'am," Erskine said and looked at Fargo. "You're their friend. Tell them what they're in for if old man Holman rides in on the prod."

"Save your breath," Phinneas told Skye as he bent to pick up his battered derby. He slapped dust off the brim and adjusted it on his head. "I know my rights under the law. And I'm not leaving Rawbone until I've helped all the people who need curing."

"Mr. Boggs—" Marshal Erskine began.

"You can save your breath, too," the patent medicine man declared. "I've been all through this before, many, many times. In town after town, from one end of the frontier to the other, I've had to put up with ridicule and abuse from drunks, skeptics, and just plain bad men. And while I'm not the bravest of men, I refuse to knuckle under, to turn tail and run like a cowardly cur." So saying, he turned and stepped to his wagon. His daughters went also to lend a hand, picking up the items scattered about.

"The darned fool," Erskine muttered, then left.

Fargo melted away, too. The crowd had pressed in closer, but parted as if by an unseen hand to permit him passage. He walked to the saloon, found the glass he'd dropped, and took it inside to the bar. On an impulse he poured another whiskey, sat at a corner table, and played solitaire for the next half an hour. Outside Boggs's voice droned on and on, but he had no urge to listen. He'd heard the same or a similar pitch a dozen times or more.

The whisper of the bat-wing doors parting snapped Fargo's head up. He thought it would be the bald bartender, but the person who waltzed in out of the baking sun had a full head of rich red hair and a voluptuous body sheathed in a tight blue dress. She took one look at the bar, halted, and blurted, "What the hell? Isn't anyone here?" She raised her voice. "Gordon, are you in the back?"

"If you mean the barkeep, he's out listening to the greatest patent medicine man in the history of civilization," Fargo said, tossing a black ten onto a red queen.

The woman gave a nervous start and faced him. "I didn't see you there in the shadows, mister," she said. "New to town, ain't you?"

Fargo nodded once and played another card.

Folding her arms across her highly developed bosom, the redhead sauntered over. "Is that what everyone is doing down the street? There's a medicine show in town?"

"You missed their grand entrance?"

"When I'm asleep, I'm dead to the world," the woman responded and put a hand to her raspberry lips to stifle a tiny yawn. "I work nights and sleep in late most days."

"Better hurry, then," Fargo advised. "You can still be cured of whatever ails you."

She grinned and said, "I'm healthy as a horse, thanks." Her voice dipped suggestively. "And some say that riding me is like riding a thoroughbred. I take a man to the finish line in style."

Fargo leaned back and gave her cleavage the sort of look a hungry man would give twin loaves of bread. "I have no doubt you do."

"The name is Wendy. Short for Wendolyn."

"Buy you a drink?"

"Does a bear like honey, honey?" Wendy made for the counter. "But you stay put. I'll help myself and bring a bottle for both of us."

Fargo felt a stirring in his loins as he watched her curvaceous backside sway across the floor. Since he was staying over so he could make a fresh start at dawn anyway, and since the sisters would be unavailable, he figured he might as well make the best of the situation. She was on her way back when someone else barreled through the doors in a bustle of excitement.

"Look at this!" the bartender, Gordon, cried happily, waving a jar filled with brown liquid. "After all these years I won't be any different from everyone else!"

"What are you babbling about?" Wendy asked.

"This!" Gordon reiterated, waving the bottle while tapping the label. "Boggs Hair Tonic and Rheumatism Cure."

"It does both?" Fargo and Wendy asked at the same time.

"Sure does. Professor Boggs concocted it himself from rare and exotic plants imported from South America," Gordon said. "Those were his exact words."

A cloud darkened Fargo's face. "Can I?" he asked, holding out his hand.

Gordon hesitated, treating the bottle as might a man holding a valuable treasure. "All right. But be careful, mister. This is the last bottle the professor had."

"How much was it, if you don't mind saying?" Fargo inquired. The cork stopper reeked of alcohol. And at the very bottom swirled minute bits of . . . something.

"Only ten dollars," Gordon said. "Usually it goes for fifteen, but the professor discounted it just for me."

"He's a saint," Fargo said, his sarcasm lost on the thrilled barman. Handing the bottle back, he rose, saying to Wendy, "Keep my seat warm for me, gorgeous. I won't be long."

"Where are you going?"

"To have a little talk with my friend the professor," Fargo said. Ears burning with anger, he marched out into the bright sunlight and up the street to where fully half of Rawbone still listened, engrossed, to Boggs ramble on. He slanted to the left, making his way around to the back side of the wagon.

"Who among us hasn't had a cold at one time or another?" Phinneas was saying. "Why, we all have. Come winter and nine out of ten of you will suffer from the sniffles, sore throats, and congestion. But not if you have a bottle of Boggs Cold Cure and Pimple Remover. For eight measly dollars— that's right, folks, only eight—you can be free of colds for as long as my sterling elixir lasts."

Fargo stepped around the corner. Phinneas was inside, leaning on the swing-out panel, waving a shiny bottle of his miracle cure at the fascinated citizens of Rawbone. In front of the wagon Liberty and Belle were selling other bottles just as fast as customers came forward with the money.

"That's it, friends," Phinneas said. "Don't be shy. It isn't wise to pinch pennies where your health is concerned."

Soundlessly, Fargo slipped inside and grasped Boggs's elbow. "We have to talk, Professor."

"What?" Phinneas started and glanced around. "Oh, it's you, sir. Can't it wait until we're done here? I have a few nostrums left to sell yet."

"Now," Fargo growled, propelling the patent medicine man into a corner.

"Am I imagining things or are you upset?"

Fargo pushed Boggs against the wall. "I don't like being lied to or played for a fool."

"What on earth are you talking about?"

"You told me that you were on the level," Fargo said. "You claimed that you're not in this business to fleece people out of their hard-earned money."

"And I told you the Gospel truth."

"Like hell you did," Fargo rasped. "Hair tonic and rheumatism cure? Cold cure and pimple remover? You're selling nothing but cheap whiskey mixed with bits of grass, bark, and colored water."

"I resent your accusation," Phinneas declared. "I've made it as plain as I possibly can that I'm not a flimflam man. You saw for yourself how much time and effort I put into preparing my medicines." He paused. "Or hasn't anything I've said or done meant a thing to you?"

Fargo said nothing.

"That's it, isn't it? You don't believe a word I've said. You really believe I'm a confidence man."

Before Fargo could answer, Belle peered inside. "Pa? Skye? What's the matter? We need more Cold Cure and Pimple Remover out here."

"I'll take two bottles!" someone was shouting.

"So will I," said a woman.

Shaking his head in disgust, Fargo retraced his steps to the saloon. Why should he meddle, he asked himself, when the fine citizens of Rawbone were all too willing to part with their hard-earned money? Just as his personal affairs were no business of the marshal's, it wasn't any of his business if Rawbone's population didn't have brains enough to see they were being swindled. And if Marshal Erskine came down hard on Phinneas and the sisters, well, that was too bad, but they were getting their due for fleecing a flock of idiots.

Wendy was at the card table, wrapping up the game of solitaire. She brightened on seeing him and remarked, "I didn't rightly know if you'd come back."

"Told you I would," Fargo said. Without thinking, he raised the whiskey bottle and took three long swallows, gulping searing mouthfuls that made his eyes water and his throat constrict.

"Whoa there, partner," Wendy said. "You planning on riding out of town with nothing but a head?"

"It wouldn't be the first time," Fargo said gruffly.

The redhead shrugged and resumed her solitaire, absently humming a tune.

"Let's dance," Fargo said. He pulled her out of the chair and pressed her firm body against his, then held her right hand out to one side and moved off across the floor.

"What in the world has gotten into you?" Wendolyn asked. "Are you mad at somebody?"

"No." Fargo whirled her in a graceful circle and saw the bartender staring at him as if he'd just downed locoweed.

"You can't fool me, mister," Wendy said. "Something is stuck in your craw."

"Be quiet and dance."

Wendy tittered, then cackled, then danced as if they were at a fancy dress ball and she was the belle of the hour. Throwing back her head, she swooped and spun with childish glee. "You're real light on your feet for such a big man," she commented after a while.

They had been dancing cheek to cheek. Fargo looked at her, saw a hint of something in her eyes that inspired him to kiss her lightly on the mouth. She gulped, licked her lips, and whispered, "Damn, you work fast."

"Your place? Or is there a hotel?" Fargo asked.

"So soon? The night is still young. And I haven't had a bite to eat since yesterday."

"Gordon!" Fargo called. "Do you serve food?"

"The tastiest vittles this sides of the Mississippi. Steak, mountain oysters, and prairie strawberries are my specialty."

"Bring them on. Two helpings, piled high."

Wendy made a change. "I'll pass on the mountain oysters, thank you very much. I'm not about to eat anything that's hung from the underside of a bull."

They sat down, and Wendy told Fargo the story of her life. How she was married at sixteen, heading west from Ohio three years later. How her husband died of disease on the trail, leaving her stranded, practically penniless, forcing her into saloon-life in order to make ends meet.

Fargo had heard her tale many times before. Countless pilgrims from back east headed west, thinking they were going to find the promised land and live happily ever after, but all they wound up with was an early grave and an unmarked makeshift cross as a testament to their foolishness.

Gordon, the bartender, was as good as his word. The meal he fixed was delicious, the steaks just right, the oysters fried to perfection, the beans seasoned to make them even tastier. Fargo gorged himself. It was the first real meal he'd had since taking the trail to Texas and the last he'd enjoy until he reached the Lone Star State.

Wendy did justice to her portions. She loosened up more and more as the meal went on, so by the time they were done, she was leaning on Fargo's shoulder and playing with his ear. "I thank you, mister, from the bottom of my heart. Most of the Scrooges who come in here don't want to buy me a drink, let alone a full meal."

"Do you want anything else?"

"Mercy, no. Another bite and I'd explode." Wendy traced a finger from his ear to his neck. "Now about that invitation. I have a place above the general store. It's not much, but it's comfortable. There's stairs and a door at the back so I can come and go as I please with whoever I please and not have the church-going ladies up in arms."

"Then let's go." Fargo took her arm, paid the tab, and strolled outdoors where the sun hung above the western horizon, blazing the sky red, orange, and pink. The activity at the wagon had tapered off. Boggs and his daughters were dealing with the last few customers, while up the street Marshal Erskine hovered, waiting for the other shoe to drop.

Fargo started to step out from under the overhang when Rawbone thundered to the driving beat of shod hooves. He pulled Wendy back into the shadows, watching a large group of riders enter the town from the east. At their forefront rode Johnny Holman. Beside him rode a man with white hair and weather-beaten features, dressed in range clothes. He had the predatory air of a hawk about him in the imperious way he regarded everything and everyone in his path.

"Why, that's old Cull himself," Wendy remarked. "Haven't seen him in Rawbone in a spell."

Fargo retreated farther into the doorway and put a finger to her lips when she went to protest. The riders trotted past without noticing them. Johnny Holman was glaring at the wagon, his features twisted in savage anticipation.

"It looks like that patent medicine man is going to wish he'd never heard of Rawbone," Wendy said. "What do you suppose is the matter?"

"Stay here," Fargo said, moving along the wall. "This doesn't concern you."

"But it does you?"

Fargo thought of Belle and their lovemaking, and of how Liberty tended his wound, and he answered, "Yes. Damn it all. I guess it does."

The few citizens near the wagon scattered as the Holman outfit fanned out and closed in. Phinneas Boggs faced around, his daughters moving to his side.

Of the seven men with Cull and Johnny, not one bothered to look over his shoulder or check on either side of the street. They were overconfident, certain no one had the gall to meddle in anything Old Man Holman did.

From behind dozens of windows curious faces peered out. The street itself was deserted save for those in the very center and Skye Fargo, who worked along until he was abreast of the wagon and could hear everything that was said. So far Cull Holman had just locked eyes with the patent medicine man in a silent battle of wills Phinneas couldn't hope to win. At length Boggs averted his gaze, and Old Man Holman smiled.

"So you're the miracle worker?"

"I heal people, sir. Miracles are the province of the Almighty."

"Healed many, have you?"

"Thousands."

"And your cures always work?"

"Most of the time. I'm not infallible."

Johnny Holman squirmed in the saddle. "Why the hell are you wasting words on this peckerwood, Pa? I told you what happened. We should run this bastard out of town and burn his wagon, then find that big son of a bitch who slugged me when I wasn't looking."

"Be patient, son," Cull said.

"Easy for you to say," Johnny replied. "You're not the one with the sore jaw."

Belle suddenly shouldered past her father and placed her fists on her hips. "This sorry excuse for a son wouldn't know the truth if it jumped up and bit him on the rump," she said defiantly. "*He* was the one who started it. He was the one who grabbed my pa and would have beat him silly if not for our friend."

From all that Fargo had heard about Cull Holman, he expected the old man to fly into a fit over having his son insulted. Fargo stepped out from under the overhang, still unnoticed by any of the riders, stopping when the elder Holman looked down on Belle in amusement, not anger.

But if Cull saw humor in her accusation, Johnny Holman did not. "Are you just going to sit there and let her talk about me like that?" the younger man growled.

"What would you have me do? Gun down a woman?"

"No. Her pa. She won't act so uppity if we shoot off a couple of his toes to put him in his place." Grinning, Johnny sneered at her. "Ain't that right, bitch?" Then, like a striking rattler, his hand stabbed for his revolver.

6

Skye Fargo knew what the younger Holman was going to do before Holman did it. Two long strides brought him close to the horsemen, and he drew at the very instant Johnny did. His Colt cleared leather first, the hammer clicking back before Johnny's six-shooter was half drawn. And almost at the same moment there was another click, to the right, and he glimpsed Marshal Erskine at the mouth of a side street.

Neither fired, though. It wasn't necessary. For as the younger Holman had drawn, the older Holman had twisted and backhanded Johnny across the face so hard Johnny toppled to the dusty ground. Dazed, the young man gawked at his father. "What did you do that for?" he demanded, a hand to his face.

"You'll throw lead when I say to and not before," Cull said. "This man is unarmed, and only a coward puts a bullet into someone who can't defend himself."

"But Pa . . ."

"Shut up," Cull ordered. "I didn't come into town to kill this healer. I came to talk business."

Johnny Holman wasn't the only one bewildered by the news, Fargo saw. Phinneas and the women exchanged puzzled glances and Marshal Erskine's brow was knit as he slowly holstered his pistol.

Fargo didn't lower his Colt until positive the younger Holman would obey Cull. He heard Phinneas clear his throat and observed him beam like a condemned man given a new lease on life.

"Business, sir? I take it you're afflicted with an ailment no one has been able to cure?"

"You take it wrong, medicine man," Cull Holman stated. "I want to know if you can fix my daughter."

"Oh, Pa," Johnny said.

"Your daughter?" Belle spoke up.

"Her name is Sarah," Cull said. "My wife died giving birth to her. She was the apple of my eye when she was little." His grating voice softened. "Then one day about two years ago she had a riding accident. Fell, hit her spine on rocks. She hasn't been the same since."

"You've taken her to a doctor?" Phinneas inquired.

"Hell, I've taken her to six doctors. Some as far off as New York. They all say the same thing." The fire in Cull's expression dimmed. "Her nerves were damaged, or some such. They all claimed she'd never be able to walk or ride again."

"So you'd like me to cure her," Phinneas said.

"I've tried everything else. Might as well try patent medicine." Cull leaned forward. "But I'm warning you here and now, mister. You'd better not string me along. If you can't help Sarah, you say so right up front. Otherwise, try to trick me, and I'll let Johnny here do as he pleases with you and your pretty girls. Come what may."

A warm hand slipped into Fargo's and the musky scent of Wendolyn's perfume engulfed him. "Thought I told you to wait at the saloon," he said.

"I was worried about you, handsome. You got me in the mood, and I'd hate for anything to spoil it."

Old Man Holman had dismounted and was chatting with Phinneas. Near as Fargo could tell, there was no need for him to hang around. Lacing arms with the redhead, he made for the general store. The sisters were so involved in the talk, they never spotted him.

Twilight was descending as the sun set. The threat of gunplay over with, Rawbone's residents resumed their normal lives, some coming out to sit on rockers and enjoy the cool evening breeze.

Fargo paid them little mind. He had a gorgeous woman beside him who was chomping at the bit to bed him, and he could think of no better way to spend the next four or five hours. Then he'd sleep like a baby until dawn and be on his way to Texas.

Some men stood in front of the saloon. Fargo thought he spied a vaguely familiar face, but when he focused on them, he didn't recognize a single one. His arm around Wendy's shoulder, they walked into the narrow gap between the general store and a frame house. At the rear, stairs led to a small landing.

Wendy fiddled with her bag, rummaging for a key. "I know the blamed thing is in here somewhere," she said.

"We could do it now," Fargo teased, gripping her smooth buttocks and rubbing his manhood against them. She giggled, wriggled, then pretended to be outraged and slapped his wrist.

"Behave yourself! Someone might see us and the next thing I know Erskine will show up and give me twenty-four hours to get out of town. Wait until we're inside."

Accenting her point, a shadow flitted across the alley. Fargo stood back, arms folded, and played the proper gentleman until she opened the door and stepped inside. Then he took a bound, snatched her around the waist, and ground his hardening pole into her posterior.

"Lord, you're a randy one," Wendy said softly, closing her eyes and matching him motion for motion.

Fargo cupped her left breast with one hand, the junction of her thighs with the other. A moan flitted from her lips, and her belly heaved from a spasm of coarse excitement. Fargo nuzzled her long hair aside to kiss the back of her neck. Her skin smelled of powder and soap.

"Is this what eating mountain oysters does to a man?" Wendy joked.

"You should see what happens when I eat the whole bull," Fargo responded.

The redhead laughed and pressed on the hand rubbing her breast to heighten her thrill. "Why don't you let me go into the bedroom and change, lover? This is the best dress I own, and I'd hate to tear it by accident."

"You don't have to go to any bother on my account," Fargo said, his finger massaging the furnace between her legs.

"Please," Wendy purred. "I'll make it worth your while."

Loathe to release her, Fargo gave her nipple a tweak, then swatted her on the fanny. "Make it quick," he urged.

"Will do." Wendy pranced to a doorway, paused, and winked seductively. "Be a dear and close the door. Throw the bolt too. We don't want any of my friends walking in on us." She blew him a kiss as she disappeared.

Fargo turned to the door and grasped the latch. Outside a

gray shroud covered the town. Soon the gray would change to black, and the night life of Rawbone would be in full swing. So would he, in a manner of speaking. The thought made him grin.

Pushing the door shut slowly, Fargo felt it bump the toe of his left boot. He shifted his leg and glanced down to verify the door would clear his foot. At that moment the tranquil town was rocked by the blast of a rifle in the alley, and the edge of the door exploded in a shower of slivers.

Fargo hunkered down, the Colt flashing into his hand. More shots cracked. Slugs tore through the door above his head and into the jamb. In the bedroom Wendy yelled, but Fargo didn't answer. He was flinging the door wide and springing onto the landing.

A vague figure flew toward the alley entrance, levering rounds frantically, firing three more times.

The shots smacked into the railing and the top step. Fargo dived flat, both arms level. He realized the man limped as he squeezed the trigger. His assailant clutched at his side, tripped, and plowed into a stack of empty wooden crates. The crash must have been heard from one end of Rawbone to the other.

Fargo went down the steps three at a bound, leaping over the last five in a long, soaring hurdle. His soles stung as he landed. Then he darted to the left, to the wall, hunkered low, and ran to the scattered jumble of crates. He expected to find the killer unconscious or dead behind them. Instead he saw scuff marks where the rifleman had dragged himself to the mouth of the alley—scuff marks bordered by fresh drops of blood.

Racing to the street, Fargo stopped shy of the corner. He poked his head out and saw residents huddled close to buildings. At the far end Marshal Erskine approached on the run.

"He went thataway!" an elderly man shouted, pointing. "Into the saloon."

It was Gordon's place, the saloon where Fargo had met Wendy. Cocking the Colt, Fargo sped to the near corner, heedless of a yell from Erskine. There should be sounds coming from within, voices and laughter and the tinkle of the tinny piano. Yet the whiskey mill was as quiet as a tomb.

Fargo had a hunch what would happen if he barged in

through the bat-wing doors. Turning, he dashed to the rear of the establishment, hoping there would be a back door.

There was, and it hung open a crack. Old boxes and crates had been stacked in untidy rows around it. Fargo wound among them and placed his ear to the crack. Was that a whisper he heard, or was it his imagination? He tested to see if the hinges would creak by moving the door an inch. When they worked noiselessly, he slipped inside.

A narrow hall smelling of food and alcohol brought Fargo to a small kitchen. A coffee pot bubbled on the stove. A newly baked apple pie rested on a counter. He cat-footed to the door beyond. Another, shorter, hall connected to the saloon.

Gordon was the first man Fargo spied. The bartender had his back to the hall, his hands lying on the counter, his body tense as wire. Past Gordon were several tables. At a couple of them card players sat in oddly frozen positions, some with cards in hand. But they weren't looking at the cards. They were looking at the right corner of the bar.

Fargo crept forward in a crouch. He dared a peek and set eyes on the ambusher.

It was the third hardcase from the dry wash, the man who had been with Jeb and String Bean. He looked the worse for wear with a bright red splotch on the right side of his shirt and the dried blood from an old wound on his left shirtsleeve. A rifle lay on the floor next to him. A pistol, a long-barreled Remington, was cocked in his right hand and pointed at the entrance.

"Somebody go take a gander out the door," the man commanded in a strained voice. "See where he is."

"Forget it, Blackwell," said one of the card players. "Ain't one of us wants to get his head shot off on your account."

"That so, Frazier?" Blackwell responded, aiming the Remington at the man who had addressed him. "Then you got a choice to make. Either get your ass out of that chair and take a look-see for me and maybe get a bullet in the brain, or sit there and definitely get one in your innards."

"Damn your hide. You have no call to make me do this," Frazier said. "I've never done you no wrong."

"Doesn't much matter at this point." Blackwell wagged the Remington. "Just do it."

The card player rose, then froze. Everyone heard rapid footsteps bearing toward the bat-wings. As one the patrons ducked under tables or hit the floor.

Blackwell aimed at the middle of the doors. The smug smile he wore indicated he assumed the runner had to be Fargo.

Fargo knew better. It was the marshal, and unless Fargo did something, Erskine would blunder into a hail of lead. Fargo propelled himself into the open, but as he swung outward, the bartender began to back up. Taken unawares, Fargo rammed into Gordon's legs, jarring the barkeep against the bar, rattling bottles from one end to the other. The jolt threw Fargo off balance, and he toppled onto his rear.

The killer had caught the motion and whirled. Wounded he might be, but Blackwell was a seasoned gunhand. His turn and the snaking whip of his arm were smooth, precise. A shade faster and he would have fired first.

But it was Fargo who squeezed trigger, firing between his upright legs, the muzzle so close to his crotch it left powder marks on his pants. The slug nailed Blackwell in the chest and flung him into the wall. Feebly, Blackwell tried to rise and shoot. Fargo's second shot cored his eyeball, and he slumped, lifeless.

A cloud of gunsmoke hung in the cramped space behind the bar as Fargo stood. Gordon and many of the customers were pale as ghosts. The bat-wings crashed wide and in burst Erskine. The lawman looked right, looked left, saw the body in the corner, and lowered his pistol.

Fargo walked over to the body, pried the Remington from its grasp, and set the revolver on the bar. "Where's your partner?" he wondered aloud. "Waiting his turn?"

Erskine leaned on the counter and gave the dead man a look of contempt. "Riding the owlhoot trail always has the same end." He glanced at Fargo. "What is it with you, mister? You've only been in Rawbone a few hours, and already you've been mixed up in more scrapes than most people see in a lifetime."

"He started it," Fargo said flatly. "I was minding my own business, and he tried to put windows in my skull."

"Was he one of those gents you mentioned, the ones giving the medicine man a hard time?"

Fargo nodded.

"Figures. He's been Baxter's riding pard for years." Erskine thoughtfully stroked his chin. "If Baxter is alive, odds are he'll make a play himself soon."

"Good."

"Good?"

"I want to get it over with."

The marshal picked up the Remington. "I know the feeling. When a man knows someone is gunning for him, he walks around on a hair trigger, a bad itch between his shoulder blades all the time." The Remington went under his belt. "Better you than me."

"Thanks a heap."

"Don't take it personal." Erskine squatted next to Blackwell. "By rights I should run you out of town. The last thing I need is more gunplay. But for reasons of my own, I won't object if you stick around a while."

"Come morning and your precious town will be nothing but a memory."

Erskine studied him a moment. "You might be happy to hear that your friends can stay as long as they like, too. Cull Holman and that Phinneas feller are being right neighborly to one another."

"They're not my friends," Fargo said, striding for the door.

"But I thought you told me—" Erskine began.

"I don't care what I told you," Fargo replied on reaching the bat-wings. He didn't bother to explain their betrayal, how he'd trusted them, taken them at their word, accepted them as honest. He didn't let the marshal know that he now believed Phinneas and the women were selling bogus cures. Erskine would find out soon enough, in a few days when the residents of Rawbone awakened to the same fact and demanded he go after Boggs and get their money back.

A small crowd had gathered. Fargo strode through them like a mountain lion through a pack of sniveling coyotes. He saw Wendolyn waiting at the alley. She rushed to meet him, taking his hands in hers.

"Thank God you're all right! I was so worried. What happened? All that shooting, and then I came out and found you gone!"

"It's over," Fargo said, encircling her waist and leading her away. "Let's take up where we left off. The night is still young."

"But what happened?" Wendy repeated. "Was someone trying to kill you? Where are they now?"

"Dead."

"You?"

"Me."

"Sweet Jesus."

Wendy fell silent until they were safe in her lodgings with the door shut and bolted. Then she folded herself into his strong arms and nibbled playfully on his chin. "Seems to me you could use some cheering up. As my granny used to say, you've got a norther riding your nose."

Fargo had never heard that one, and he chuckled. The yielding softness of her breasts and thighs stirred his loins. Combined, they did wonders for his disposition. He chucked his hat onto a table, unhitched his gunbelt and draped it over a chair, and pulled off his boots.

"I'm glad you have manners," the redhead commented. "Some of the yacks I bring up here keep their damn spurs on and rip my bed sheets all to hell." She noticed the ankle sheath. "My, my. Aren't you plumb full of surprises. What's the pigsticker for, scratching your back?"

"Sticking pigs," Fargo said, removing the toothpick and setting it by his hat. He hitched at his pants, loosening them so they fell about his shins.

Wendy's eyes became as big as walnuts, and she hungrily licked her lips. "You really *are* full of surprises! Haven't seen one that size in a coon's age."

"Any complaints?" Fargo pulled her closer.

"Are you kidding me, handsome? I live for loving." Features lined with growing lust, Wendy gently took his manhood in her hands and fondled it like a solid gold staff. "Ohhhhh. I died and went to heaven, and no one thought to tell me."

Fargo gripped her curly mane, tangling his fingers in the strands, as she lowered her head. An exquisite sensation coursed from his groin to his spine to his brain. Throwing his head back, he closed his eyes and groaned. She knew just what to do to drive him to the heights of passion. His loins became living fire, his blood molten lava.

Wendy made slurping and gulping sounds, her lips and tongue working in a masterful combination. Meanwhile, her fingers cupped him from below and massaged lightly.

It went on like this for the longest while, until Fargo realized if it went on any longer he wouldn't be able to contain himself. He stepped back, sliding from her mouth. She pouted a moment, then cheered when he knelt in front of her and hitched at her dress.

"Oh, you naughty boy!"

Fargo pried her lacy underthings apart like the petals of a rose in order to gain her fragrant core. His tongue moistened her inner thighs as he nuzzled his way higher. When it brushed her slit, she cried out. He wedged his nose into her nether lips and licked greedily.

Wendy rocked on her heels, her knees buckling, then recovered and clasped both sides of his head so she could grind him deeper into her. She groaned, and kept on groaning, doing so each time he licked her passion knob.

Bracing her marble smooth buttocks with both hands, Fargo steered her toward a settee. She guessed his intent and sat down slowly, parting her legs wider to grant him easier access. Her feet went over his shoulders, her heels dug into his back.

Fargo wormed his mouth from side to side, making her pant. Reaching up, he squeezed her ripe breasts, the nipples like rocky spikes under his palms. She humped wildly for several seconds, stiffened, and gushed. Her womanly scent seemed to float on the air.

"Oh! Oh, yesssssss!"

Laying her flat, Fargo swiftly unfastened the top of her dress, yanked the folds to either side, and clamped his lips on her right breast. His right hand stroked her down under. She arched into him, her hips working of their own accord, building the friction to a fever pitch.

First one breast, then the other, claimed Fargo's attention. He liked to rub their rounded contours and suck on her big nipples. She had dabbed powder on them earlier, and Fargo swore he smelled the fragrance of pine.

The settee creaked underneath them as Fargo leaned back on his knees. He ran the tip of his member across the tip of her womanhood. Wendy gulped, grasped his wrist, and said, "Put it in! Please! I'm ready!"

Her slick inner walls confirmed it. Fargo buried himself to the hilt, inch by gradual inch, tiny stabs of pleasure lancing through him. When all the way in, he paused to prolong the inevitable, and she tried to spur him into action with her tongue and her nails. He held back, though, as much for her benefit as his.

Wendy had a way of moving her bottom that would send any man into fits of delirium. Fargo could only resist so long, and then he just had to begin the ages-old rocking-horse motion that would eventually carry them to the peak of bittersweet physical delight. Again and again he pounded into her. Again and again she thrust as he pounded.

The climax was a long time coming. By then they were caked with perspiration, and her groans were loud enough to be heard down in the general store, but she didn't seem to care and neither did he.

Fargo went faster and faster, trying to fulfill her before slipping over the edge himself. He thought she might be one of those women who took forever, but at long last Wendy whined and shook and spent, which was his cue to do the same, except for the whining. His well-muscled frame quivered from head to toe as he spurted deep into her. She clung to him, and for that moment in time and eternity they were one.

Afterward, Fargo lay on top of her and drifted asleep, lulled by the release and her warmth. Later that night he awoke, carried her into the bedroom, and made love to her again. They slumbered side by side, his arm draped across her. Twice he awakened, once when she stirred and mumbled, smacking her lips as if eating food.

The second time was an hour or two after dawn. Fargo awoke to see pale sunlight in the window and wondered what had brought him around. He didn't wonder long as the next second a rifle barrel appeared in front of his startled eyes and a voice he knew greeted him.

"Rise and shine, feller. And no quick moves or else."

Fargo sat up, pulling the rumpled sheet high enough to cover himself. "What the hell!" he declared.

"I won't ask twice," Marshal Erskine warned, leveling his rifle.

And so did the five other men in the room.

7

Cull Holman sat in a great mahogany chair in the lavish living room of his huge house and studied Skye Fargo as an eagle might eye succulent prey just before plummeting from the sky and breaking the prey's back with a vicious snap of its steely talons. "So this is him?" he asked no one in particular.

"It sure is, Pa," Johnny Holman said from his post slightly behind the chair, and to one side. "It's the same one who hit me, who knocked me down."

Old Man Holman glanced at Marshal Erskine. "Where did you find him?"

"Wendy's. Just like Gordon said we would."

"He give you a hard time?"

Fargo had about reached the limits of his patience. He'd been furious at being rousted out of bed without an explanation, his fury simmering as he was hustled into his clothes and pushed out to the street where the lawman had the Ovaro waiting. Now, ringed by the men who had brought him to the Holman spread, and others, the chair containing the lord of Rawbone only a few feet away, he took a step and growled before Erskine could reply, "Not yet, I haven't. But if I don't get some answers soon that will change."

Pistols whipped from holsters. A few rifles were trained on him. Cull Holman sat there as calm as could be and gestured at the gunmen, stilling them. "Take a look around you. In case you haven't noticed, you're in no position to threaten anyone."

"Looks can be deceiving."

The younger Holman patted his six-gun. "Let me have him, Pa. Me and a few of the boys will beat some respect into the jackass."

Cull slowly shook his head. "Not this one, son. Something

tells me this one is as tough as they come. Beating on him would do nothing but make him madder than he already is."

"Who cares?" Johnny responded sullenly.

"*You* should," Cull said. "How many times have I told you that the key to success in this life is being able to read people like you would a book? Look at him!" Cull speared a finger at Fargo. "He's not a pampered brat like you. And he's not your run-of-the-mill drifter or cowhand. This one has sand, boy. Enough to fill a desert."

"If you say so, Pa."

Old Man Holman sighed, then faced around. "What's your handle, mister?"

"Skye Fargo."

"Fargo?" Cull repeated. "I know that name. Where have I heard it before?" Forehead creasing, he placed an elbow on the polished arm of the chair and started to prop his chin in his hand. Suddenly he gave a little jerk and slapped the arm, hard. "Fargo! Of course! The scout? The tracker? The one folks call the Trailsman?"

Fargo merely nodded.

"This doesn't make any sense," Cull said harshly to the lawman. "A man like him in cahoots with them?"

Erskine had acted like a man slapped in the face on learning Fargo's identity. Then he'd smiled as if pleased at learning a fact he'd suspected all along. Now he said, "I never claimed any such thing. All I know is that Fargo rode into town with them. When I talked to him, I got the impression they were friends of his. And when trouble brewed he was right there to help them." Erskine paused. "But later he told me they weren't his friends and got riled when I tried to find out more."

"What the hell is this all about?" Fargo cut in. "Boggs and his so-called cures?"

"So-called?" Cull slid to the edge of his chair. "Do you know something we don't?"

"All I know is that I'd better get some answers, and pronto," Fargo said.

Johnny hissed and made like he was going to come around the chair and wade into him. "Nobody talks to my pa that way, mister!"

"Pipe down, damn it," Cull snapped. He bowed his head a moment and rubbed his eyes, the raw iron willpower he radiated seeming to drain from him like water down a drain, and for all of ten seconds he was no more or less than a weary old man who had apparently not slept a wink all night and who was in the grip of severe emotional turmoil.

The sight dampened Fargo's fiery anger as nothing else could have. He wouldn't forget the way he had been treated, nor Wendy being pushed roughly to the floor when she tried to stop the men from taking him, but he decided to hold his temper for the time being, to learn what was behind all this. Then he would act, and those who had to pay, would.

"I have a daughter—," Cull said softly, straightening.

"Sarah. I know. I heard you tell Boggs," Fargo said.

"Then you know I'd do anything to see her well again. Even consult a patent medicine man when simple horse sense tells me I'm wasting my time." The old man folded his hands on a knee. "Boggs and I had a long talk last night. He agreed to try his best to cure her, but only if I paid a hefty fee."

Fargo would have throttled Phinneas if the man was standing in front of him.

"Our agreement called for me to pay him half the money in advance, the other half once Sarah can walk again," Cull detailed. "So last night I gave him two thousand dollars."

"Which is probably more money than he's seen at one time in his whole life," Fargo commented.

Old Man Holman frowned. "Evidently so. Because at sunrise this morning I sent two men to escort Boggs here, as we'd agreed, and he was gone. Him, and his daughters, too."

"You shouldn't have any trouble catching him in that wagon," Fargo said.

"How true," Cull said. "Unfortunately, his wagon is right where he parked it yesterday. No, it seems Phinneas Boggs broke into the livery late last night and stole three horses. By now he and his girls might be halfway to Texas for all I know."

The light of understanding made Fargo nod. "So that's why you sent the marshal after me."

"Yes. I had hoped you were in league with Boggs and you'd be able to tell me which way he'd gone. But it's obvious I was mistaken." Cull Holman rose and held out his hand. "I'm sincerely sorry, Fargo. For what it's worth."

By the stunned looks on most of those present, Fargo gathered that Old Man Holman had never apologized for anything, ever. He shook and saw relief in the other man's eyes.

Holman coughed, then said, "Now that we have this little mix-up out of the way, I'd like to make you a proposition. They say you're the best damn tracker since Daniel Boone. Maybe you'd let me hire you to track down Boggs?" His son muttered, but Cull ignored him. "I want him bad, Fargo. For getting my hopes up the way he did, I want to see him get his due. So I'm willing to pay you five hundred dollars."

Someone whistled. Fargo had to agree the sum was a lot for a simple tracking job, and under different circumstances he would have accepted, gladly. "I'll hunt them down, but you keep your money."

"You'll do it for free? Why?"

"Let's just say it's personal and let it go at that."

Johnny Holman snorted. "You can't trust him, Pa. I think he's stringing you along so those others can get clean away."

"No, he won't," Marshal Erskine butted in. "I'd stake my badge on it."

The father put a hand on his son's shoulder and said, "When the Good Lord handed out brains, you were in the outhouse. Let me do the thinking, boy. You go to the corral and have nine fresh horses saddled."

"But pa—"

"Just do as I say." Cull waited until Johnny was gone, then said to Fargo, "We can leave within the hour, if that's all right with you."

"We?"

"I'm the one Phinneas Boggs swindled. So I'm tagging along and taking seven of my hands and the marshal with me."

Fargo saw Erskine open his mouth to speak, think better of the idea, and fall silent. "I can make better time by my lonesome," he pointed out.

"No doubt. But I need to be there when you overtake him," Cull said. "I want to see his face when he comes to realize he'll be spending the next ten years in prison."

Premonition prompted Fargo to say no, to insist on going alone. The appeal on the old man's face gave him pause, though, and he reluctantly said, "Fair enough. I'll be ready to leave by ten." Turning, Fargo walked over to the man holding his Sharps, Colt, and toothpick, the very same man who had shoved Wendy. "I'll take my hardware now," he said.

The man looked at Cull Holman, who nodded. "Here you go," he said, holding out the Sharps. "No hard feelings, I reckon?"

Fargo waited until he had the rifle in hand before answering, "You reckon wrong." And with that, Fargo hauled off and slugged the man in the stomach with the stock, driving it in so deep the man collapsed like a punctured balloon, his breath whooshing out of him in loud gusts. Spinning, Fargo covered the others in case they cared to make an issue of it.

"No gunplay!" Cull roared as several of his men coiled. "Any *hombre* who touches his pistol answers to me!" Advancing, he confronted Fargo. "Was that necessary? What did Weldon ever do to you?"

"He likes to push women around," Fargo said, retrieving the Colt and toothpick. No one objected as he strapped both on. He verified the Colt was loaded, deftly spun the cylinder, and twirled the pistol into his holster.

"You're handy with a gun, too, I see," Cull remarked.

"I'll be back by ten," Fargo said, pushing through the men blocking the front door. "Be ready."

Walking out into the blistering heat of the day was like walking into a furnace. Fargo squinted in the harsh sunlight, stepped into the stirrups, and trotted toward Rawbone. While he had no call to doubt Old Man Holman, and while he no longer felt obliged to look after Boggs and the women, he wanted to check Holman's story. He wouldn't put it past someone as high and mighty as Cull to use him for his own selfish ends if it should serve Cull's interests.

The first stop was at Wendy's. Fargo rapped on the door, and it was jerked wide to reveal the redhead with a slab of raw meat pressed to her left eye.

"Skye!" Wendy cried, forgetting herself and throwing her arms around him. The entire left side of her face was terribly swollen, the eye the worst of all. "I was afraid Holman was fixing to string you up!"

"Last I heard, a man can't be hanged without a trial," Fargo mentioned, sorry he hadn't pounded Weldon into the floorboards.

"The finer points of the law have never stopped Cull before.

Trust me, that man has his own way whether anyone else likes it or not."

"A point to keep in mind," Fargo said. Pushing her back, he examined her despite her embarrassed protests. "I didn't figure Weldon shoved you this hard."

"He didn't," Wendy said. "I was running down the stairs after them, and I tripped over my own big feet." She pressed the meat to her eye and flinched. "Fortunately Gordon heard all the fuss and ran over. He gave me this piece of steak."

"Seen or heard anything of the patent medicine man?"

"There's a story going around that he skipped town with a lot of Old Man Holman's money." Wendy shook her head in disbelief. "I wouldn't have thought anyone could be so stupid. Cull will eat them alive."

"Could be." Fargo kissed her forehead, then stepped to the doorway. "Take care of yourself, Wendolyn."

"You're leaving? For good?"

"I'll be passing through on my way back from Texas. If you want, I'll look you up."

The redhead smiled wanly. "I'll be counting the days, handsome. Don't you disappoint me, you hear?"

Fargo's second stop was at the livery, which was run by a swarthy man wearing a *serape*.

"*Sí, señor*," he responded to Skye's question. "I came in this morning and found three of my best horses gone. Someone had kicked in the back door and taken them out the same way. Stole three fine saddles and bridles, too, that didn't belong to me. Now the men who lost them are demanding I make good their loss." He rolled his dark eyes. "What did I do to deserve this, eh?"

"You say the door was kicked in?"

"*Sí*. Part of the wood splintered. I must replace the door also. As if I do not have enough—"

"Did anyone see it happen?" Fargo interrupted, unwilling to listen to the stableman recite his woes.

"No, *señor*. The marshal, he asked around, but no one even heard it."

"Thanks for the information." Mounting, Fargo rode to the rear of the livery. The door hung on one hinge, bits and pieces lying on the ground. So many people had been there since the

75

break in that any tracks left by the culprits had long since been obliterated.

Fargo went around the corral and crossed a field to an isolated stand of oak trees. The earth was hard-packed and dry, not at all the kind likely to bear prints, but he found a few anyway, partial tracks that told a story in themselves. Interesting, he mused. Did it mean what he thought it meant? Or was a new element involved? Perhaps someone working with Phinneas of whom he knew nothing?

The general store was his third stop. Here Fargo stocked up on the few items he needed for the trail. And, as a precaution, he bought insurance against treachery.

It was nearing ten when Fargo galloped into Cull Holman's yard. The old man, the marshal, and seven riders were set to leave. So was someone else, Johnny Holman.

"See, boy?" Cull gloated. "I told you Fargo is a man of his word. You've got to learn who to trust and who not to trust or you'll never amount to a hill of beans."

"I try my best, Pa," Johnny said.

"Sometimes our best just isn't good enough, son. We have to do better than our best."

"Whatever you say."

The idea of spending several days with the bickering Holmans was enough to give Fargo second thoughts. But as the cagey old man had noted, Fargo had given his word. He was committed. "Everyone set?" he asked curtly.

"Loaded for bear," Cull said. "How about you? You don't seem too eager to take part."

"I told you. I'd rather do it alone." Fargo wheeled the Ovaro, and in doing so his gaze drifted to a window on the second floor of the grand house. There, bathed in sunshine so that her face seemed to shine with an inner light, sat a pale young woman maybe two years Johnny's junior. Her arms and legs were sticks, her body wasting away from a lack of exercise. She struggled to lift a thin hand and waved her scarecrow fingers weakly in parting, "Cull," Fargo said, nodding.

Old Man Holman looked and blanched. He waved back, smiling broadly while gurgling as if he had something stuck in his throat. "Sarah," he whispered, seemingly afraid she would hear. "My sweet Sarah."

Fargo saw Johnny's eyes mist over, then the younger Holman spurred his sorrel past the pinto. Fargo followed, and one by one the rest of the hunting party fell into line. And it was just that, Fargo realized—Cull Holman's private hunting party.

Taking the lead, Fargo galloped toward Rawbone, angling toward the stand of ashes once they came into sight. Cull Holman caught up with him, but had no comments to make until they reached the trees and Fargo was circling to pick up the trail.

"You think they came this way?"

"I know they did."

"Is that where you took off to? You did some scouting around?"

A clod of overturned earth was the clue Fargo sought. He reined up and stared hard at the elder Holman. "Before we go any farther, there are a few things we have to settle."

"Such as?" Cull asked distrustfully.

"Such as who's in charge," Fargo said. "So long as we're on the trail, I am."

"Now just hold on—" Cull protested.

"It's not open for debate," Fargo warned. "Either my say-so is the only one that counts or you can try and track them down yourselves."

Johnny had the look of a cougar about to spring. "I knew it, Pa," he snapped. "I knew he'd do something like this."

Coals burned in Old Man Holman's eyes. "Why this sudden interest in being top dog?"

"It's not sudden," Fargo said.

"Why?" Cull persisted. "What difference does it make? Are Boggs and you on friendlier terms than you've let on? Are you afraid I'll lynch him the moment I get my hands on him?" He speared a thick finger at the marshal. "Hell, why do you think I insisted Erskine come along? He wouldn't let me turn vigilante. But I reckon you know that."

Fargo had to admit the argument had merit. The marshal was on Holman's leash, sure enough, but he'd seen for himself there was a line Erskine wouldn't cross. The lawman wouldn't abide cold-blooded murder, as he'd proved when he'd been set to stop Johnny from gunning down Phinneas. "Doesn't matter," he answered. "From this point on I call the shots or I don't go. That's the deal. Take it or leave it."

It was Johnny who spoke next, but Fargo knew his father was thinking the same thing. "And what's to stop us from agreeing now and then doing as we damn well please later on?"

"Your word."

Cull Holman shifted in his saddle. Fargo waited, knowing he had them between a rock and a hard place. They couldn't track Boggs down without him. Holman had to agree or let the patent medicine man get clean away. "Well?" Fargo goaded.

"You're a hard man, mister," Cull said bitterly.

Fargo knew why the old man was hedging. In the West a man lived, and often died, by his word. A promise given was gospel, a man's word his bond. A man only had to break it once to earn a reputation as an unreliable liar. And for someone like Cull that was unthinkable.

"All right, damn you," Old Man Holman said. "You run the show until we get back to Rawbone. I'll do as you say." He leaned forward. "But just don't push me too far, Trailsman. Or I'll make you live to regret it."

"All I care about is getting at the truth," Fargo said.

"What does that mean? Boggs stole my money. It's as simple as that."

"We'll see," Fargo declared. Lashing the reins, he headed for the rolling forested hills stretching in unending green waves to the horizon. Many miles beyond that horizon lay Texas. Coincidence, Fargo reflected? No, the shattered door was proof to the contrary.

For the next several hours Fargo held to a steady, brisk pace. At a ribbon of a creek he stopped briefly to water and rest their mounts. He sipped a handful and was adjusting his cinch when the marshal appeared on the other side of the Ovaro.

"All the stories they tell about you aren't lies," Erskine said. "You're some tracker. I know, because I've done some tracking myself. And there's no way in hell I could follow the trail as fast as you're doing."

"I've had lots of practice."

"And you must have the eyes of a hawk," Erskine said, scanning the glade. "I've looked and looked, and all I've seen are a few smudges here and there. This ground is hard, but it's not *that* hard. There should be more tracks."

"There would be, except they tied burlap bags over the hooves of their horses back at the ash stand," Fargo said.

The lawman mulled the news a bit. "How do you know?"

"I saw a pile of old bags out behind the livery. Someone had gone through them, picking out the ones without holes, I figure. The owner was so upset about the stolen horses and saddles, he never noticed." Fargo finished with the cinch and lowered the fender. "Then there were faint tracks leading into the stand but only those smudges afterward." He reached in a pants pocket and produced a short length of twine. "Plus I found this among the trees."

"I'll be damned."

Cull and Johnny had been listening attentively.

"I don't like you keeping important information all to yourself," Old Man Holman said. "Are there any other secrets we should know?"

"Just one," Fargo said.

"When are you planning to share it?"

"Now is as good a time as any." Fargo walked to the creek and halted where a muddy bank sloped into the sluggish water. "See anything?"

Erskine squatted to closely examine the spot. "I see footprints," he said. "They all took a drink here before they moved on." He touched two different sets of small, slender tracks. "These were made by the women, Belle and Liberty." His finger went to a wider set. "This must be Phinneas." Then the marshal did a double take and indicated another pair of prints, deep and wide like Boggs's but several inches longer. "Look!" he exclaimed. "There's another man with them!"

"That's right," Fargo said.

"What the hell!" Cull barked. "You've known all along and haven't told us?"

"He's real smart, Pa," Johnny said caustically. "Why, he's so damn smart, I bet he knows who this other *hombre* is."

"Do you?" Cull demanded.

"I can guess," Fargo said, gazing in the direction the quartet had taken. "Whoever stole the horses kicked in the stable door. Phinneas couldn't do it if his life depended on it, and the women weren't strong enough either. It had to be some-one big and powerful—someone who didn't care about break-ing the law." He looked at each of them. "Someone like Jeb Baxter."

8

They covered several more miles before Cull asked the question uppermost on all their minds. "Why did Baxter do it? Erskine told me that you tangled with him a while back. And I heard all about your shootout with Blackwell. Is there a connection?"

"Must be," Fargo said.

"Do you think Boggs and his girls went willingly?"

Fargo had pondered the same question for some time. He couldn't see Phinneas going to church with Baxter, let alone going off into the wilderness and allowing the women to go along. "No," he said honestly.

"Do you realize what you're saying?" Cull spat in annoyance. "I might be wrong. Maybe the medicine man didn't steal my money. Maybe Baxter has him at gunpoint." Another thought jarred the old man. "The sisters! Baxter can do as he wants with them, hide the bodies so no one will ever find them, and ride off without a care in the world."

"Not if we overtake him first," Fargo said.

Cull grumbled a few words, then stated, "Any man who will hurt women doesn't deserve to live. I've done some things in my time that I'm not proud of, things that would get me hung if I did them today, but I never harmed a hair on the fairer sex, never hit a kid or rode a horse to death or kicked someone when he was down." He cocked an eye at Skye. "You savvy?"

"You're a man, not an animal," Fargo said. Despite himself, he was growing to like the old cuss. There was more to Cull Holman than met the eye. "Which is more than can be said about Baxter."

"What is it with the young ones nowadays?" Cull mused. "In my time men were hard as nails. Had to be to survive. But we weren't vicious like some of them are today. We didn't kill folks for the sheer fun of it, didn't go around stealing and maiming for lack of something better to do." He slapped at a buzzing fly. "They're just plain vicious."

"Mad dogs," Fargo said. "And there's only one way to deal with a rabid animal."

Cull grinned. "You'll do to ride the river with, Trailsman. We're more alike than you might think."

In a short while they came to a clearing where the burlap bags had been removed and cast aside. Talking became impossible. Fargo wanted to overhaul Baxter by nightfall and to that end he brought the stallion to a gallop and never slowed once during the next hour.

The tracks showed they were gaining, but not as rapidly as Fargo hoped. Jeb Baxter was a shrewd judge of horseflesh and had stolen the best animals in the livery. From the sign, Fargo could tell Baxter was pushing hard, whether to put as many miles behind him as he could before dark or out of haste to reach a specific destination, Fargo had no idea.

The sun sank lower and lower. Fargo glanced at it often, his concern growing as the shadows lengthened. He began to think he would have to track at night using a torch, never easy to do and a dead giveaway if the torchlight was seen, when the tracks revealed the quartet had finally slowed to a walk.

Fargo immediately reined up. They were descending the slope of a small hill. Below reared dense woodland. A barren clearing stood out like a glaring brown hole in a green carpet, about a quarter of a mile away. That was where Baxter would camp for the night, Fargo guessed.

"Are we close?" Marshal Erskine asked.

"Close enough," Fargo said, shucking the Sharps. "We go on foot from here. Leave one man with the horses."

The forest was deathly quiet. Fargo heard no birds, no squirrels, not even any insects. Their presence alone could not account for the stillness. Something else had driven the animals silent. But what?

Fargo stayed on the trail until he glimpsed the clearing ahead. Stopping, he motioned, and the rest of the men spread out. He moved into the brush, placing each foot carefully, avoiding twigs and snags.

No scent of woodsmoke hung on the evening air. No sounds

greeted Fargo's ears, no low voices or horses nickering or anything that would confirm Baxter had indeed made camp for the night. Then a single noise did break the hush, a drawn-out, faltering groan, so laden with pain it brought goose bumps to Fargo's skin and reminded him of the time he discovered a hapless prospector who had been skinned alive and staked out on an ant hill by Apaches.

Fargo went faster, the Sharps wedged to his shoulder. He drew close enough to see all of the clearing, to see there wasn't a fire, wasn't a string of tethered horses. But there was someone lying in a puddle of blood, a crushed black derby beside him.

In long strides Fargo hurtled from cover. He stood over the patent medicine man and marveled that anyone could take so much punishment and still be alive.

Phinneas Boggs had been pistol whipped. Not once or twice, as happened to rowdy drunks when they bucked a town marshal. Boggs had been hit so many times his face was crisscross with bloody, swollen welts. His flesh resembled a plowed field more than human skin. In addition his nose was broken, his eyes swollen nearly shut, his lips split, his front teeth broken.

"Good God!"

The rest of the men had gathered around. Cull looked shocked. Johnny looked queasy. Marshal Erskine's lips compressed in a thin red slash.

Kneeling, Fargo gently rolled Boggs onto his back. Blood drenched his white shirt, caked his throat. Scores of rips in the fabric showed his chest and arms had been whipped, too, his arms no doubt when he tried to protect himself from the blows. Fargo looked at Boggs's hands. Several fingers had been broken and the knuckles were horribly puffed up.

"Scum," Old Man Holman said. "Vile, despicable scum."

No one had to ask who he meant. Fargo leaned down to whisper, "Phinneas? It's Skye Fargo. Can you hear me?"

Boggs groaned again. His eyelids quivered, as if he was trying to open them wide but couldn't. He made a gurgling sound, a strangled, "Llllarrgo?"

"Yes," Fargo confirmed. "Be still. We'll tend you, get you back to town where the sawbones can doctor you back to health."

Phinneas whined, then gestured frantically.

At first Fargo didn't understand, not until he saw where Boggs was trying to point. "You want us to keep going, to save Belle and Liberty?"

The lacerated head bobbed.

"I'll find them," Fargo said. "First things first, though."

Boggs sobbed pathetically, tears trickling from the bloated lids covering his eyes. He wouldn't stop gesturing, wouldn't stop whining.

Cull Holman broke the spell. Whirling, he snapped orders like one born to command. "Danton, fetch Troy and the horses. And be quick about it. Bill, you start a fire. Johnny, you and the rest go into the woods and find enough limbs to make a travois—"

"A what, Pa?"

"A litter like the Indians use to haul their kids and whatnot. You've seen them. This man is in no shape to ride and won't be for days. So we'll drag him all the way to Rawbone if need be."

Everyone dispersed. Fargo walked to the southeast side of the clearing. Bending to touch a track, he ran some of the dirt through his fingers. It was loose and slightly cool, as it would be if Baxter had ridden on less than an hour before.

Less than an hour, Fargo reflected, but it might as well be a year. The sun had vacated the sky and night was coming on apace. Gloom pervaded the forest, darkening by the moment. To continue tracking he must resort to a torch, which an alert man like Baxter would spy a long way off. Baxter would know someone was on his trail and flee, perhaps slaying the women first so they wouldn't slow him down. As much as Fargo hated the notion, he had to wait until dawn.

Marshal Erskine was doing his best to make Phinneas Boggs comfortable. He had removed his jacket, folded it, and placed it under Boggs's head for a pillow. Now he was using a white handkerchief to wipe blood from Boggs's face. He looked up as Fargo came over and said softly, "He'll live, I think, but he'll be bedridden for weeks. Maybe months."

The patent medicine man was unconscious, breathing noisily through his tumorous mouth.

"We'll send two men back with him," Cull said. "The rest of us will push on at first light and not rest until those poor women are safe." He glanced at Fargo and added, "That is, if it's all right with you?"

Before Fargo could answer, Marshal Erskine gave a cry of surprise and pulled a hand from one of Boggs's pockets.

"Look at this, Cull! Your two thousand dollars."

Old Man Holman snatched the wad of money and gaped at it in amazement. "What the hell!" he blurted. "I figured this would be in Jeb's poke."

"He must not have known Boggs had it," the lawman speculated.

"All Baxter wants is the women," Fargo said grimly, and the other two men glared into the twilight.

Presently the horses arrived. By then the fire blazed high, and Cull gave orders for water to be heated in a coffeepot. Enough straight limbs were collected to start work on the travois.

Fargo knelt on the other side of Boggs and helped Erskine clean the wounds and apply splints to Boggs's broken fingers. Phinneas groaned and tossed, mumbling constantly, his fever worsening.

An hour later they had done all they could. Both men sat back, the lawman pushing his hat back to wipe a sleeve across his perspiring forehead. "I wonder what did it," he said, half to himself.

"Did what?" Fargo asked.

"Drove Jeb Baxter over the edge. He's always been a curly wolf, but he was smart enough not to bare his fangs in Rawbone. I figured he knew better."

"There isn't a wolf alive that will sit still for a leash. Sooner or later it will bite the hand holding the leash and run off to live wild and free."

"I suppose," Erskine said. "Whatever the reason, Jeb has bought himself a prison stretch or a necktie social, whichever the judge decides."

"Unless he can reach the Badlands," Fargo said.

"Damn. Hadn't thought of that."

But Fargo had. The Badlands were a bleak, arid section of country shunned by everyone except reptilian and human sidewinders. Bad men of every kind went there to escape the long arm of the law, particularly Texas bad men. They'd rather live with the ever-present threat of rattlers and Comanches than do a strangulation jig under the limbs of a Texas cottonwood.

The word "Badlands" had an unforeseen effect on Phinneas. His eyes cracked open and he tried to sit up. Erskine held him down, advising him to lie still, but Boggs twisted his head and fixed those horrid slits on Fargo.

The swollen lips moved, croaking words barely audible. Fargo had to bend closer and listen hard to understand the distorted sounds.

"My guurls!" Phinneas said.

"Baxter still has them, but not for long," Fargo vowed. "You should rest, conserve your strength."

"Mushhht save . . . " Phinneas gurgled, sputtering. "Mushhtt! Mushhht!"

"I will," Fargo said.

"Nowr! You mushhtt go nowr!"

"It's too dark to track," Fargo explained. "I have to wait until daylight."

"No, no." Phinneas shook his head. "Plleasshh! Go Nowr! Carnn't let . . . dem . . . take . . . dauftters!"

"Them?" Fargo said.

Phinneas tried to nod, the movement making him whimper. He reached up awkwardly, trying to grab Fargo's arm, but the splints on his fingers kept him from getting a grip. Tears seeping from the corners of his eyes, he tugged weakly at Fargo's wrist.

"Calm yourself, feller," Marshal Erskine urged. "We'll have your daughters back in town, safe and sound, by tomorrow night, the next morning at the very latest."

"No," Phinneas blubbered, his eyes not leaving Fargo. He held both hands up and tried to cup them, as if to beg. "Go nowr," he said laboriously. "Nowr!"

"He can't," Erskine said. "It's too dark. Can't you tell?"

Fargo put his hands on Boggs's shoulders to push Phinneas onto his back, but Boggs resisted, the tears gushing in a torrent. Suddenly Fargo understood there was more to the desperate pleading than the love of a father for his offspring. There was something else, some underlying horror that Phinneas was trying to get across to them. "What is it?" he asked. "Why must I go right this minute?"

Boggs worked his lips slowly. "Cccom-an-chair . . . ssss."

Gibberish, Fargo thought. Perhaps he was wrong. "Try again. I don't understand."

Phinneas bowed his head and blubbered. Sniffling, he spoke as distinctly as he could. "Com . . . an . . . chair . . . ooosss."

"He's talking nonsense," Erskine remarked. "The sentence makes no sense."

"No!" Phinneas wailed. "No! Com . . . an . . . chair . . . oooos! Com . . . an . . . chair . . . oos!"

"Lie down," Erskine said. "You're only making yourself worse. Whatever it is can wait until morning."

"No, it can't," Fargo said, because he had abruptly realized Phinneas was saying a single word, not a whole sentence. Piecing the syllables together, he said gravely, "Comancheros."

"Oh, Lord," the lawman said.

From Cull Holman came a sharp intake of breath.

Just mentioning the despised name of the Comancheros was enough to chill the soul of any man who had lived in the Southwest for any length of time. Fargo knew how widely hated they were from his wide-flung travels. They were considered as bad as the Comanches, with whom they traded.

Most Comancheros were half-breeds, combining Indian blood with either white or Mexican, and were shunned by Indians, whites, and Mexicans alike. To make a living they had taken to being go-betweens. Whenever the Comanches raided in Mexico and brought back plunder, the Comancheros would arrange to sell the goods to whites for top dollar. Or when white captives were being ransomed, it was the Comancheros who made the arrangements.

There was more. Everyone knew the Comanches were fond of taking white wives. And everyone suspected the Comancheros of supplying such wives, although as yet no one had been able to prove it. Every so often, though, the wife of a rancher would disappear while out for a ride, or a woman would disappear while hanging her laundry to dry on the outskirts of a town, and the Comancheros would be suspected.

"Jeb Baxter plans to sell your daughters to the Co-mancheros?" Fargo said to Phinneas.

Boggs nodded, slumped, and openly wept, his shoulders shaking uncontrollably.

"Did he say he knew where to find a Comanchero camp?" Fargo probed.

The patent medicine man nodded while crying in great racking sobs.

"Where is it, Phinneas?" Fargo asked.

"Doornn't knowr," Boggs wheezed.

"Do you have any idea how close it is?"

"No." Phinneas lifted his head. "Clossshh, dough. Werrry clossshh."

"That can't be," Erskine said. "We're two days shy of the Badlands yet. And the Comancheros hole up deep in there, maybe a four- or five-day ride. That's a whole week, all told."

"Closshh," Boggs insisted in his mockery of a voice.

Standing, Fargo cradled the Sharps in the crook of his left elbow and walked toward the pinto. He did not need to turn to know who fell in step beside him.

"You can't go by yourself," Cull said.

"One man stands a better chance of taking him by surprise than eight would."

"But it's dark. What can you hope to accomplish when you can't even see their tracks?"

"I'll find a way," Fargo insisted. He jammed the rifle into its scabbard, forked leather, and tapped the brim of his hat. "Take good care of Boggs. I hope he can help your daughter when he's well."

"You make it sound like we'll never set eyes on you again," Cull said.

"If it's meant to be, it's meant to be," Fargo said, riding to the southeast. Trees closed around him, surrounding him with ranks of ghostly gray sentinels, and in his mind's eye he saw them as hordes of bloodthirsty Comancheros. Shaking his head to dispel the images, he skirted a walnut tree.

It was child's play to tell direction at night. All Fargo had to do was find the two stars forming the front of the Big Dipper. They pointed right at the North Star.

Since Jeb Baxter had been heading due southeast from the

moment he left Rawbone, Fargo counted on the hardcase continuing to do so. He rode slowly, stopping repeatedly to rise in the stirrups and study the lay of the land. If luck was with him, he would spot Baxter's campfire—provided Baxter had made one. A canny hardcase like the Texan might decide on a cold camp, in which case he might pass within a few dozen yards of where they were and never know it.

Fargo recollected that Baxter had left Phinneas for dead about an hour before sunset. How far would Baxter have gone afterward? At a trot Baxter could have covered four or five miles before darkness set in. Allowing another mile or two for twilight riding, and the farthest Fargo figured he should have to go was seven miles.

Estimating distance at night was a lot harder than telling direction. Lacking landmarks to judge by, Fargo had to guess based on how far he *felt* he'd gone. He had a fair idea of when the first mile fell behind him, but after that the distance blurred into itself.

He stopped once and glanced over his shoulder. The glow from the fire was a glaring beacon in the midst of an inky sea. Jeb Baxter might have seen it and be flying toward Texas like heel flies were after him.

Normal night sounds accompanied Fargo as he rode on. His right hand resting on the Colt, he went down a hill, followed a winding basin to a tableland and climbed to the top for a bird's-eye view. The sight of a fire half a mile or so off sent a tingle of excitement down his back. He'd found them!

Fargo picked his way forward with the utmost care. The breeze might carry any sound, however slight, to their camp, alerting the Texan. And he must not let Baxter get away again.

A quarter of a mile from the dancing flames Fargo dismounted and tied the stallion to a tree. He didn't like leaving the Ovaro. There were too many mountain lions and bears prowling the hills. Yet he dared not risk having the horse step on a twig or make some other noise.

Fargo took the Sharps although at close range, at night, the Colt was more effective. He removed his spurs and stuffed them in a saddlebag. His bandanna he pulled up to his nose to reduce the amount of pale skin showing.

The undergrowth was dense here, requiring Fargo to make

many detours. When the brush formed a solid wall, he crawled, avoiding areas littered with fallen branches.

At last the individual flames were clear enough to see. Fargo sank to his stomach and wormed around a thicket. He was twenty yards from the camp and as yet had not observed anyone moving about. He hoped the sisters were asleep and Baxter was drowsing by the fire.

Fargo swung to the east. If he were in the Texan's boots, he'd be facing northwest so he could watch his back trail. By stalking the camp from the east, he should be able to catch Baxter off guard. He wouldn't try to take Jeb alive, wouldn't yell at him to throw up his hands or else as Marshal Erskine would do. No, Fargo would simply take deliberate aim and put a bullet in Baxter's brain. And that would be the end of it.

The flames were slowly dying, which was encouraging, Fargo thought. Baxter must be asleep. He spied a log ahead, very near the clearing. Lying flatter, he snaked to the log inch by slow inch. Once there he listened for the longest while, hoping to hear snoring, the rustle of clothes as someone tossed about, but the sole sound was the crackle of the fire.

Fargo raised his head high enough for his eyes to clear the log. For half a minute the glare of the flames obscured everything else. Then he was able to make out several lumpy shapes, the bundled forms of the sisters and the Texan. But which was which?

Two of the sleepers were beside one another. The third lay a few yards off. Fargo deduced this last must be Jeb. Yet he dared not shoot without being one hundred percent certain. And there was just one way to verify the truth.

Shoving upright, Fargo vaulted the log and sprinted madly toward the blankets. He thought for sure Baxter would hear him and leap up, and then he could fire without fear of accidentally hitting the women. But not one of the sleepers moved.

Blood pounding in his temples, Fargo reached the third bundled shape and kicked with his right boot to send Baxter rolling. To his astonishment and dismay, the kick merely collapsed the blanket in upon itself, several long sticks poking from underneath. Like a fist to the face, the truth made him re-coil.

No one was there.

It had been a trick.

Jeb Baxter and Belle and Liberty were long gone.

9

The first pale pink hint of impending dawn lined the eastern horizon when Fargo stepped into the saddle and resumed the chase. He was now racing against time itself. He had to catch the Texan before the Texan reached the Comancheros, or saving the sisters would become next to impossible.

Fargo searched the clearing and soon found the trail. The tracks did not bear to the southeast as they always had before. Baxter had gone due south, which would bring him to the Badlands territory that much sooner.

He clucked the Ovaro onward and swallowed the bitter bile that rose in his throat at the thought of being outfoxed. Somehow, Jeb had discovered there was a posse in pursuit. The wily varmint had rigged the fake camp to divert and slow down his pursuers, and Fargo had fallen for the ruse like a rank greenhorn.

Fargo had been forced to spend a fitful night resting in order to be refreshed enough to take up the trail again the next day. Sleep had been a long time coming, though, and hard to enjoy; Fargo was too concerned about the women. Were they strangers it would be a different story. His feelings wouldn't enter into the picture. But he knew the sisters well, had made love to one of them. Their abduction was a personal thing.

As yet there was no change in the rolling, forested countryside. That would change before the day was out. Fargo glimpsed a doe bounding in flight into the brush and his stomach growled. Food would have to wait, he decided. There would be plenty of time for a roast haunch of venison once the women were safe.

Fargo figured Baxter would not have gone far before making his real camp, so Fargo kept seeking the charred remains of a fire. As mile after mile was covered and no such evidence appeared, he realized he'd been outsmarted twice. The Texan had not stopped at all, but had ridden on through the night. By now Baxter must be very close to the Badlands, and before noon would be in them.

There were two choices, as Fargo saw it. He could ride back to get the marshal and Old Man Holman, losing more time in the bargain. Or he could press on alone and trust in his ability to get the women out of the fix they were in before either of them lost their lives or suffered a fate much worse than death.

Time was the factor that made Fargo's decision for him. He trotted on over hill after hill, the trees thinning as the morning waned, the woodland broken by dry patches of grass that became more and more frequent.

Toward noon Fargo came to a small spring. The tracks revealed the Texan and the women had stopped for a brief rest sometime during the night. He would rather keep going, but he had the pinto to think of. Water would be almighty scarce in the Badlands. Better to let the Ovaro drink its fill now, he reasoned.

Twenty minutes later, Fargo was on the go again. After two hours dry, flat grassland had replaced the rolling hills. Four hours later the first eroded butte towered in the distance like some ungodly sculpture crafted by a loco artist.

The grass faded to dry soil before long. Heat rose from the rock hard ground in a scorching, shimmering wave. The country ahead was utterly lifeless, as dry as a desert, as foreboding as a grizzly's gaping maw. The Badlands were aptly named.

Tracking was harder to do. The prints were fewer, the impressions not as deep. Fargo was able to ride at a fast clip, but not as fast as previously. He imagined the sisters must be worn to a frazzle and envisioned Baxter prodding them on with cuffs and curses.

Buttes reared in increasing numbers, mingled with larger mesas, spiny switchbacks, and high peaks pointing stony fingers at the sky as if in bitter accusation. The temperature, impossibly, seemed to soar. Sweat poured down Fargo in a slick sheet and he removed his bandanna to dab often at his neck and face.

Fargo had seldom felt so completely alone. Accustomed as he was to traveling by himself through long stretches of pristine wilderness, it was nothing like being the sole moving figure amidst a vast, bleak landscape as deathly still as a cemetery, the hot air searing his lungs as would the brimstone air of hell. After a while he came to feel like he was the only living creature in the world.

The tracks proved otherwise. And like a tenacious bloodhound Fargo dogged those tracks as the afternoon waxed and the feverish sun arced to the west. Evening found him at the base of a ragged peak, no water anywhere to be had, and the Texan still miles ahead.

Fargo reined up, slid down, and sat on a flat boulder. His body craved rest, but his mind refused. He would ride on for as long as he could without risk of losing the trail, confident Jeb couldn't ride through the night two nights in a row. Or even if Jeb could, Liberty and Belle couldn't.

A lone star gleamed like a tiny jewel in the dark blue sky when Fargo mounted. Miles off a high ridge formed a knobby black backbone, and it was toward this the tracks led him. He looked forward to reaching the top, for from there he might at long last catch his first glimpse of the three he sought if Baxter had scraped together enough wisps of vegetation to build a fire.

The ridge proved farther off than Fargo thought, and he had to remind himself distances were deceiving in the Badlands. The dry, clear air magnified everything, making far-off objects appear a stone's throw away.

It was past nine by Fargo's reckoning when he reached the bottom of a winding narrow trail that led to the crest. The trail bothered him. It shouldn't be there. Since it was, it meant someone used it on a fairly regular basis, and there were only two possibilities. Comanches or Comancheros, or both. Yet neither were known to come this far north. Comanchero country lay two days south, maybe three.

Fargo put the mystery aside as he climbed. As he neared the top, he straightened, eager to spot Baxter's camp. A sluggish breeze fanned his head and shoulders once he cleared the rim. He looked out over the Badlands, twisting from side to side, unable to hold back an oath of frustration.

There was no fire.

Fargo slumped in the saddle, feeling as if he had let the sisters down. They must spend another night in Baxter's less than charming company, and he could only pray Baxter was too tired from two days without sleep to pester them much. But then, Baxter *was* a Texan.

The breeze refreshed Fargo after the day of baking heat. Since he had no inkling of the direction Baxter took at the bottom of the ridge, and since in the morning he'd be able to see for miles from his vantage point, Fargo made a cold camp there. He stripped off his saddle and saddle blanket, unrolled his bedroll, and was asleep moments after closing his eyes. Only once did he stir, when the wind brought a faint, quavering cry to his ears. He sat bolt upright, unsure of whether he'd heard a coyote or a woman's scream. For a long while he listened, but never heard it again.

Before dawn Fargo was saddled and scouring the Badlands below. Nothing moved in the wasteland, not so much as a solitary buzzard. He could see the tracks of three horses, appearing like tiny bird tracks from that height. They went straight south, ever deeper into the heart of hell.

Fargo descended, then brought the Ovaro to a brisk walk, the fastest he could ride in the terrible heat. This would be the day he caught them. He could feel it in his bones. He forged steadily on across the unending nightmare domain until the sun was half way to its zenith. Then, after so long, he spotted something else that moved, another living thing. More than one, it turned out. There were six buzzards soaring low on the sluggish currents, circling a specific spot.

Images of Belle and Liberty suffering the same fate as their father sparked Fargo to a gallop. More buzzards took angry wing as he approached something lying on the dusty earth. From several hundreds yards off he recognized the outline of a fallen horse. The last vulture flapped into the sky, hissing like an enraged snake, as he halted.

The cause of death was as plain as the nose on Fargo's face. The animal had been ridden into the ground. Its mouth and chest were flecked with dried tendrils of white foam, its features locked in the haggard stare it had worn at the moment of keeling over. It explained how Baxter was able to keep ahead of Fargo. And it inspired Fargo because it meant the other two horses must be in a sorry state, close to dropping dead themselves.

"We have them," Fargo told the Ovaro and gave the stallion a pat. He bypassed the dead animal so the stench wouldn't bother the pinto. Once in the clear he ate up the miles, six of them by midday.

The terrain began to change. Steep cliffs cut by ravines and gorges crisscrossed the region in a bewildering maze. The tracks curved at random, avoiding obstacles, always following the easiest route. The splay of dust ringing each hoof showed that Baxter had not slowed down after losing the horse. If anything, the Texan had picked up the pace. One of the remaining mounts, the one carrying double, showed signs of flagging.

An idea occurred to Fargo, one he dismissed as unlikely. Yet as the hours ticked by with agonizing slowness, he began to think the idea wasn't as preposterous as he supposed. Why else would Jeb Baxter push his animals so severely?

Then, toward the middle of the afternoon, Fargo reached a gap through which those he trailed had passed, and there in the dusty earth were other tracks over which Baxter's horse and the sister's animal had ridden, hoofprints recently made, indicating a large body of horsemen had gone through not long before the Texan.

Fargo halted to give the Ovaro a breather and to scan the heights on either side. He saw no one, nor did it seem likely they would have a lookout posted. Not here in the Badlands, where only outlaws and fools ventured.

Heading to the right, Fargo looked for another way to reach whatever lay beyond the opening. A solid rock wall hundreds of feet high denied him entrance, and after going a quarter of a mile he gave up and returned to the gap. Why deny the obvious? he asked himself. There would be only one way in and he knew it.

Unsheathing the Sharps, Fargo inserted a cartridge, propped the stock on his left thigh, and went in. The gap narrowed, the walls closing in on him until they were so close he scraped his stirrups on the turns. Above, a fiery slash of sky sneered down as if taunting him.

Around an abrupt bend the gap ended. Before Fargo's startled gaze unfolded a hidden canyon five or six miles long and half that wide. And, wonder of wonders, vegetation grew, a smattering of trees and brush along the left side of the canyon two miles farther.

Fargo hugged the wall to his left, making for a jumble of huge boulders. The tracks all went toward the vegetation, and as Fargo studied the greenery again, he spied a thin column of smoke spiraling slowly skyward.

Once concealed from view, Fargo swung down, ground-hitched the Ovaro, and stepped to where he could see the full expanse of the hidden canyon. It was an ideal hiding place, a perfect spot to conduct business if the business was outside the law and you didn't care for prying eyes to witness your activities.

There were four hours of daylight left, at the most. Fargo hunkered down to await nightfall. As badly outnumbered as he now was, he had to outthink the opposition, not outgun them. Darkness would give him an edge, but not much of one when dealing with hardened killers who were half Indian, men who had the wilderness savvy and reflexes of their Indian fathers.

Thanks to the high cliffs, the valley cooled sooner than the outlying wastelands. Two columns of smoke were visible when Fargo crept into the nearest brush. He didn't go far at all when he heard muted voices and low laughter.

Then Fargo smelled the delicious dankness of water. It had been so long since he last drank that his mouth watered. Looking around, he saw a shoelace of a stream meandering along the base of the high walls. It rose from an underground source and flowed into the canyon, forming an oasis of life in the midst of desolation. Only Indians, or those very like Indians, could have discovered it.

Fargo couldn't resist gliding to the stream and dipping to drink. His hand trembled a bit as he cupped the cool liquid in his palm and sipped. The water had a mineral taste and a yellowish-orange tint that showed it contained iron, but after so long without, it was some of the tastiest he'd ever had.

As a wary mountain lion would do, Fargo looked this way and that as he satisfied his thirst, his eyes never still for a moment. The rustle of leaves gave away a rabbit moving through the undergrowth. Sparrows flitted about and somewhere a hawk screeched.

Staying near the water where the brush was thickest, Fargo worked westward. The voices grew louder, the stream widened. He saw figures moving about and listened to both Spanish and English being used. A patch of mesquite was all that blocked him from the encampment. Parting a thin branch, he set eyes on those Jeb Baxter had been in such a hurry to reach.

Over thirty Comancheros dotted a grassy area, some lounging in the shade, some tending stock, others talking. Their clothes varied widely. Some wore Mexican attire, including wide sombreros. Others were partial to Indian garb, including knee-high moccasins. A few dressed like whites.

Fargo felt surprise on seeing that among the Comancheros moved a dozen or so women, either Indians or Mexicans or breeds. He remembered hearing somewhere that Comancheros rarely took white wives. They regarded white women as too weak to endure the hard life they lived.

A few ramshackle shacks had been erected using whatever wood was available and crudely cut planks. They appeared as sturdy as toothpicks and would probably be blown over by the first storm that came along. The same with the dozen lean-tos. There were also five tents, the canvases patched in so many places they resembled quilts.

Fargo did not see any children, but he did count seven dogs, mongrels every bit as vicious as their masters. He kept a wary eye on them in case one should drift in his direction. Fortunately, they were content to laze about in the shade.

The ones Fargo wanted to see, he didn't. Neither Liberty nor Belle were anywhere in the camp, nor did he catch sight of Jeb Baxter. That is, until gruff laughter came through the doorway of the biggest shack and out strolled the grizzled bastard with a bottle of whiskey in one hand and his arm on the shoulders of a grimy, bearded Comanchero in a sombrero. The pair were flanked by several other members of the band.

Fargo figured the man in the sombrero was the leader. The pair walked toward the stream, laughing and clapping one another on the back, apparently the best of *amigos*. Fargo crouched lower and fingered the Sharps. Soon they were in earshot.

"—good after that long, hot ride," the Texan was saying while wiping whiskey from his mouth.

"I have no doubt, my friend," the Comanchero said. "But we have more important business to discuss, *sí*?"

"And the sooner, the better, Chavez," Baxter said. "I can't wait to get to Texas where my kin will help me lay low for a spell." He took another swig. "And I can't wait to be shy of those bitches. The both of them have more lip than a muley cow! I had to gag them after I beat their pa silly or they would have gabbed my ears right off."

Chavez laughed roughly and clapped Jeb on the arm. "Women, eh? All they know how to do is make a man's life difficult."

Baxter recoiled when clapped, wincing and grabbing at his side. "Careful there!" he barked. "I told you that Fargo character about made wolf meat of me. Another inch and I would have been a goner."

"Sorry, *amigo*," Chavez said, but he did not sound sorry.

Fargo glanced at the shacks, looking for a clue as to which one contained the sisters. It was so obvious he was surprised he hadn't noticed sooner. In front of a small shack situated under a huge elm a bored Comanchero dressed Indian fashion sat on a rickety chair, a rifle resting on his legs. As Fargo looked, the man yawned, then shook his head to ward off the drowsiness.

"Down to business," Jeb Baxter declared, taking a seat on a log near the stream. "And let's not waste each other's time, dickering. We've known each other too long for that." He jabbed a thumb at the Comanchero leader. "How much will you give me for those two beauties?"

Chavez remained standing. He idly scratched his chin, making a show of pondering the question. While he did, the three men with him slowly and quite casually moved a few paces to either side.

Fargo realized what was going to happen and tensed. He couldn't understand why the Texan didn't see it until he watched Baxter take another drink and saw the bottle was two-thirds empty already. A bottle no doubt supplied by Chavez.

"How much?" Baxter prompted when the Comanchero was slow in answering.

"Because we are *amigos*, I will give you five hundred."

"Each?"

"For both."

Baxter swept to his feet and shook the bottle in the Comanchero's face. "What the hell are you trying to pull? We both know you can get two thousand for those women. Give me a grand for all my trouble, and you'll still come out a thousand ahead."

"Five hundred," Chavez said.

"Not on your life," Baxter said.

"You need time to think the offer over," Chavez proposed. "Rest from your long ride and this evening we will talk it over again."

"I don't need no rest!" the Texan snapped. "There's no way in hell I'm turning those women over to you for five hundred stinking dollars!" He took yet another swallow, then frowned. "It's no secret you're a lying, cheating son of a bitch, but I never figured you'd try to cheat me."

Chavez looked away, as if staring into the distance, but from Fargo's hiding place he clearly saw the Comanchero's features darken dangerously.

"Because we have been *amigos*," Chavez said softly, "I will not take insult and will give you one more chance. Sleep off the whiskey, Jeb, and come see me later."

"Go to hell!" Baxter snapped, lifting the whiskey bottle one final time.

"You first, my former friend," Chavez said. He nodded curtly.

To the Texan's credit he finally awakened to his peril and made a desperate grab for his pistol. His hand was closing on the butt when three guns boomed several times apiece. Baxter jerked backward, arms flopping, wearing an expression of dumb surprise. The revolver fell from nerveless fingers as he toppled onto his back into the stream, blood oozing down his chest.

Chavez sighed, walked to the body, and gave it a nudge with his boot. "You were a fine one to criticize the pretty *señoritas* for talking too much, old friend," he remarked. "And you should have known that for so much money I would have my own mother roasted alive." Pivoting, he commanded, "Drag this pig off before he pollutes the water. Leave him somewhere for the buzzards to find." He smiled. "They have to eat, too."

Fargo was glad to see Baxter get his due. But the Texan's death didn't change anything. Somehow he still must spirit Liberty and Belle from this vile nest of vipers and get them safely across the Badlands to Rawbone.

The three Comancheros hauled Baxter from the stream, but before taking him farther, they squatted and one rummaged through his pockets while the other two stripped him down to his underwear.

Fargo gazed at the camp as the trio left. The shooting had barely caused a ripple in the activity. Some had stopped to look, then gone on about their own business. The man guarding the sisters was drawing in the dirt with a stick.

There was a window in the shack. It lacked glass and a curtain and was no more than a lopsided square cut in the wall for ventilation. At that moment a pale face wreathed in dark hair framed itself in the square.

It was Belle, Fargo realized, and involuntarily rose a few inches, wishing he had a means of signaling her to let her know he was there. Belle poked her head out and spoke to the guard who completely ignored her. She spoke again. The Comanchero glanced at her, then motioned for her to move from the window. A third time she said something, and this time the guard rose and entered the shack.

Fargo braced for a scream or violent shouts, but heard only the laughter of a portly Comanchero fondling an Indian woman. Presently the guard stepped into the sunlight and called out to Chavez, who was standing in front of the large shack.

"What is it?" the leader responded.

"They want water and something to eat. What should I do?"

"Was your mother a jackass and your father an idiot? They are no use to us dead. Give it to them, Black Bear, and don't bother me again with such trifles."

Exhaling in relief, Fargo went to sink back down and then

felt his gut tighten into a knot. He froze, not even blinking, ignoring a cramp in his lower back.

One of the camp dogs stood ten feet away, a big brown mongrel capable of holding its own against a cougar. Body rigid, tail held high, it stared straight at the mesquite. Straight at Fargo.

10

There was no denying the dog had seen him. Fargo slipped a finger onto the trigger of the Sharps and slowly thumbed back the hammer. Would the mongrel bark and give him away or not? It took several steps toward the mesquite, the short hairs on its neck starting to bristle.

That was when a Comanchero rubbing down a horse off to the right glanced up, spotted the dog, and shouted in Spanish, "*Perro!* Get over here! No more chasing rabbits and coming back all covered with burrs for you! Here! *Pronto!*"

The mongrel hesitated, uttering a confused whine. It took a half step toward the mesquite.

"*Perro!*" the man bellowed.

Head drooping, the dog trotted back to its master and was soundly cuffed for obeying, then told to lie down.

Fargo spun on a boot heel and got out of there before another dog nosed around. Midway to the boulders he stopped to drink once again, then hurried so he could bring the Ovaro to water. He should have done it sooner but he'd wanted to check on the women. Rounding the last boulder, he reached the spot where he had left the pinto and drew up short.

The stallion was gone.

Fargo scoured the ground, suspecting the Comancheros had stumbled on his mount. He found no footprints other than his own, no hoofprints other than those of the Ovaro, which led him out of the boulders on the opposite side and then around toward the vegetation.

He should have foreseen this, Fargo reflected. The Ovaro was as dependable as a horse could be, but it had been burning with thirst when they stopped and been unable to wait for him to return. Fargo tested the breeze, learned it had shifted and brought the scent of the water right to the stallion. He could hardly blame it for straying off; any blame was his for not letting it drink sooner.

Fargo raced into the trees. At the stream the tracks showed where the pinto drank for a long while and then moved on, wandering downstream toward the Comancheros. Fargo sprinted, unable to avoid making noise due to the brittle twigs and dry leaves underfoot. He caught sight of something large moving twenty yards in front of him and increased his speed.

Seconds later shouts broke out. Fargo noticed four figures crashing through the brush toward the Ovaro, which turned to run. One of the figures leaped, caught the trailing reins, and held fast. In short order the pinto was surrounded and being taken toward the camp where a commotion had broken out.

Fargo halted, thwarted. And in grave jeopardy. Chavez would take one look at the Ovaro and have every last Comanchero out hunting its rider. He must locate somewhere to hide until they called off the search.

Whirling, Fargo dashed into the stream and ran to where the water gushed out of the ground. Above him on the right loomed the cliff, not as steep here as the outer cliff and laced with cracks and defiles. He ran into one of the gullies, then worked his way up it until a sheer sheet of rock stopped him.

From the canyon floor rose shouts. A single shot rang out, perhaps a signal.

Fargo knew how a buck brought to bay by a pack of wolves would feel. He headed for the mouth of the defile, but slid to a halt on spotting forms flitting from boulder to boulder below. The Comancheros were equal to their reputation. In such short time they'd trailed him into the gorge and were climbing to find him.

Trapped, Fargo sought a way out. A narrow ledge winding upward across the rock face to his left was the only avenue of escape. He climbed as swiftly as he could. The Sharps slowed him down, but he was not about to discard it.

Someone else shouted, and a six-shooter cracked. A slug struck below Fargo's boots and rock chips flew. More shots thundered, the leaden volley pockmarking the cliff all round Fargo. By some miracle the shots missed. Someone bawled a few words, and the firing ceased.

Suddenly, the sheer wall folded in upon itself, forming a recessed shelf five feet wide. From the ground it had not been apparent. Fargo quickly slid onto the shelf on his belly and backed from the edge so no one could pick him off from below. He held the Sharps in front of him, trained on the opening.

For a few minutes no sounds issued from lower down. Fargo shifted, heard faint footfalls, then a gaggle of low voices directly under the shelf.

"Where the hell is he?"

"I know I saw him up there."

"Maybe we winged him."

"He would have fallen. You see any body, any blood?"

"Well, he couldn't just up and disappear."

There was more, but they conversed in whispers, leaving Fargo in the dark. He heard their footsteps echo in the gorge as they departed, followed by a nerve-racking quiet.

Fargo moved to the lip of the shelf. The gorge was deserted, nor were there Comancheros moving down near the stream. They had given up, gone elsewhere. Or were they trying to lure him out into the open? he wondered, and lay on his side. Right there was as good as anywhere to hide until dark, which would fall in an hour.

Yells from the canyon showed the hunt was still in progress. Fargo listened, thinking of the sisters. By now they must have seen the Ovaro. He hoped they were smart enough to stay awake and alert tonight so if he came for them they would be ready.

The change between day and night was rapid. Once the sun vanished below the horizon, the canyon was plunged into dusky gloom. Fargo began his descent when it was barely light enough to see the ledge. It took him twice as long to reach the bottom as it had to climb, and once on firm footing he swiftly regained the stream and without hesitation made for the encampment.

Several campfires blazed high, illuminating the area. Cook pots hung from tripods and were being tended by women. Only two men were present, the guard at the shack and the portly Comanchero who had not moved from the spot where he sat earlier. He appeared to be asleep.

Fargo assumed the rest of the Comancheros were off trying to find him. And while they were gone, he intended to sneak in quickly and be out again before anyone else noticed. He cautiously skirted the camp until he was lying in weeds to the rear of the shack where the women were being held.

None of the buildings were lit within. Either the Comancheros had a shortage of lanterns, or they spent their nights in the lean-tos and tents.

Kneeling, Fargo watched the women closely, and when none were facing in his direction, he bolted to the back wall. A carpenter would have laughed the builder to shame. Wide cracks separated many of the rough planks, some wide enough for him to see inside. He thought he saw someone move in the coal black interior. "Belle?" he whispered softly so the guard wouldn't hear.

No answer was forthcoming. Fargo went to the north corner, checked if the coast was clear, then slid to the next corner. Black Bear still sat by the door, his chin nodding in his losing struggle to stay awake.

Fargo looked at the cook fires and was surprised to see the women were gone. Shadows played over the insides of the tents, showing him where they had gone. Temporarily, the coast was clear. Raising the Sharps on high, he stalked the dozing Comanchero, the stock angled so he could bash it on the man's head before the man knew what hit him. He was a foot from his quarry when from within the darkened doorway came a familiar metallic click.

"Do that, *señor*, and I will be obliged to blow your brains out."

Black Bear snapped to life and swung around to cover Fargo, his smirk proof he had been shamming all along.

Any thought of trying to escape was dashed as Comancheros poured from all directions. They came from within each shack and the lean-tos and from out of the brush bordering the camp. Most had guns leveled.

Chavez strode through the doorway, a nickel-plated Navy Colt in his right hand. Behind him came others, spreading out. Belle and Liberty were hauled into the open, both bound and gagged.

Fargo slowly lowered the Sharps and had it plucked from his grasp by Black Bear. A sallow-faced Comanchero relieved him of the Colt, then frisked him but neglected to reach inside his boots.

"So," Chavez said, holstering his pistol when convinced

Fargo had been disarmed, "you are the one who gave my late friend Jeb Baxter so much trouble, yes? You are the man called Fargo?"

Skye said nothing.

"Come now," the Comanchero leader chided. "Being stubborn proves nothing. And if you anger me, I might forget myself and take out my anger on one of the lovely *señoritas*. Would you want that to happen, *Señor* Fargo?"

"No," Fargo said reluctantly. He would have given anything to be able to smash his fist into the smug bastard's teeth.

"That is better." Chavez nodded at the man who had done the frisking. "Armando, you can untie the ladies now. Have Juanita prepare my supper, and tell her I will have three guests." Chavez smiled thinly. "You are in luck, *Señor* Fargo. A while ago my Comanche friends brought me six small pigs stolen from a *rancho*. Tonight we eat the last one."

Fargo was more interested in the sisters than the menu. Belle glanced defiantly at her captors as they removed the rope binding her wrists and tried to bite the fingers of the man who removed her gag. Liberty, however, stood meekly, her dazed eyes pools of sorrow.

"After you, my friends," Chavez said in his sickingly polite manner, gesturing.

A phalanx of Comancheros escorted the three captives to a grassy knoll under a tree where a blanket had been spread. As if by magic, lanterns had materialized all over the camp, and one now hung on a low limb above the blanket. An attractive woman with hip-length raven hair was busy setting out dishes and silverware.

"Have a seat," Chavez said, dropping down, cross-legged.

Fargo wound up with a woman on either side. Behind him sat four Comancheros, each with a revolver in his lap. They were taking no chances. One false move and he'd be riddled.

"I trust, *Señor* Fargo, that you know the *señoritas*, or you would not have gone such lengths to find them," Chavez said.

"We're acquainted," Fargo admitted.

"Is one your wife?"

"No."

"A lover, perhaps?"

Fargo shook his head.

"Are you related?"

"We're friends."

Chavez arched an eyebrow. "You trailed Baxter all this way for a couple of *amigas*? Either you are the most honorable man I have ever met, *gringo*, or you are the biggest liar. Which is it?"

Belle suddenly exploded, slapping the blanket and saying, "What do you know about honor, you mangy son of a bitch? How many innocent people have you murdered in your time? How many woman like us have you terrorized?"

Fargo put a hand on her wrist to warn her to be quiet. But the Comanchero didn't become angry, as he expected. There was more to this Chavez than met the eye. And there was no denying he was one of the most deadly men Fargo had ever tangled with.

"By your standards I have done many wrongs," the leader told Belle. "By my own, I have done only that which was necessary at the time I did it." He chuckled. "Were I truly as bad as you think, I would have raped both of you by now and then let my men use you until you bled to death."

"Are we supposed to be grateful for small favors?" Belle asked resentfully.

"I merely made a point." Chavez stretched out on his side and propped an elbow under him. "And since you questioned my honor, I will be honest and tell you that to me you are trade goods, nothing more, nothing less. Beautiful goods to be sold to the highest bidder, which in your case will be the Comanches when Little Mountain pays us a visit soon. You will bring a high price," he concluded happily.

"May you rot in hell!" Belle said.

Fargo had been scouring the camp and spied the Ovaro tied with the other Comanchero mounts. The stallion must have been acting up because it was hobbled as well.

"A fine animal, but loyal to just one man," Chavez commented, having noticed. "I knew you would not leave without it." He pushed his plate toward Juanita, the raven-haired woman, who had returned bearing a pot and ladle. "I plan to keep your Ovaro for myself. A few lashes of my whip should teach it to obey."

"And me?" Fargo finally asked.

"I have not made up my mind," Chavez said. "It would be a

stupid waste to just shoot you dead as some of my men wanted to do. We have so little to entertain us as it is."

The threat seemed to hang in the air above Fargo like a knife about to slash down. He looked at the hard faces of the Comancheros glinting the color of blood in the combined light of the fires and the lanterns and swore he could see the lust for torture in their glowing eyes. Comancheros were famous for taking perverse delight in making their victims suffer in a thousand and one creative ways.

"I must give your fate more thought," Chavez was saying. "We might hang you upside down over a fire. Or peel your skin off. Or rip out your fingernails and toenails and tongue." One of his men snickered. "Or maybe we will give you to the Comanches and let them do as they please. Little Mountain does so love to kill white-eyes."

Unbidden to Fargo's mind came the memory of a cavalry officer taken prisoner by Comanches. The man had been found staked out on a plain. It turned out the Comanches had taken turns stabbing him, but never in a vital organ. It had been great sport for them, the purpose being to see how long they could stab him without having him die on them. For three days they'd had their fun, then gone on, leaving the man to his anguish. A patrol had found him, and in the middle of the night he had taken a sleeping sergeant's revolver and shot himself in the head.

Just then Liberty spoke, surprising everyone. "Ransom," she said, her voice barely audible.

Chavez leaned toward her. "Have my ears tricked me or did you talk at last, blond one?"

"Would you let us go for a ransom?" Liberty repeated, louder.

"The idea is tempting," Chavez said, "but who would ransom you, eh? It would have to be a lot of money to make it worth my while. And who do you know who has much money?" He shook his head as if in sympathy with her plight. "Baxter told me about killing your *padre*. Is there someone else who would pay money for your release?"

"Yes," Liberty said. "There's a man in Rawbone, a rich man who was friendly to my pa. He might pay."

"Might? What is this rich *hombre* called?"

"Cull Holman."

Peals of laughter burst from the Comanchero leader and most of his men. Some laughed so hard they rocked backward, holding their sides. It was more than ridicule, Fargo sensed. They were laughing as would men who were in on a joke only they shared. But he had no idea what it could be.

"Cull Holman?" Chavez said when he caught his breath. "The same Cull Holman who killed anyone who got in his way when he settled in this territory? The same Holman who had Rawbone built from the ground up just so he could have his own private town? The one who rules everyone under him with an iron fist? That Cull Holman?"

"He's not the monster you make him out to be," Liberty said.

"*Señorita*, in his own way he is more of a monster, as you call him, than I am." Chavez chortled. "You must not be in your right mind if you think a man like him would pay thousands of dollars for your safe return."

"It wouldn't hurt to send someone with a message from us." Liberty refused to buckle.

"I would be wasting my time," Chavez said. "Believe me. His reputation is well known. He would laugh harder at the note than we did at you."

Conversation was dropped as the Comancheros took their cue from their leader and ate their supper. Fargo poked at the pork and potatoes on his plate, his pride warring with his hunger. He didn't care to accept anything from the cutthroats, but he had to keep his strength up for later. With that in mind he wolfed his meal.

Afterward cigarettes and pipes were lit. Some of the women nestled in the laps of their men. Juanita perched proudly on Chavez's knee.

The sisters appeared to relax a little, to let down their guard but Fargo knew better. This was the lull before the storm. Chavez was staring at him like a cat staring at a helpless canary.

"What should we do with you, *Señor* Fargo?" the Comanchero leader abruptly asked. "I have been thinking about that all during supper."

"You leave him be, you hear?" Belle blustered. "Touch a hair on his head, and we'll give you so much trouble you won't know what to do with us."

"Please, *señorita,* do not insult my intelligence and I will not insult yours. You are in no position to make demands." Chavez thoughtfully puffed on his cigarillo. "I like the idea of giving you to Little Mountain, but I cannot give just anyone to him. It should be someone tough, someone who will not faint at the sight of his own blood." He leered at Skye. "Can you stand the sight of your own blood, my friend?"

Some of the Comancheros chuckled.

"Yes, I think I should test you before giving you to the Comanches," Chavez said. He motioned at the stars. "Besides, a little amusement is in order on such a fine night, is it not?" He looked at his followers. "Is there none of you who would like to cut this *gringo* up a little for the sport of it?"

"*Sí!*"

"Yes!"

A dozen men or more answered, and Chavez took his sweet time picking one. At length he pointed at Black Bear. "You, *amigo!* You hate *gringos* more than any of us. One shot your father, didn't he?"

The viperish Comanchero bobbed his head as might a snake about to strike.

"Do you think you can beat our guest?"

Again that serpentlike motion.

"Very well." Chavez sat up. "Pedro, we need the circle set up. *Pronto, por favor.* Jesus, the sash. Armando, the knives. Snap to it!"

The Comancheros hustled to do their assigned tasks. At the center of the camp a wide circular area was cleared. Lanterns were gathered, ten of them in all, then arranged around the perimeter of the circle at regular intervals. Their combined radiance lit up the circle as if it were daylight.

Meanwhile the man named Jesus jogged to a tent and presently came back holding a long, frayed red sash that once might have been part of the uniform of a Mexican military officer.

At the same time Armando went to a lean-to. On his return he held gleaming Bowies in each brawny hand. The knives were an expensive matched set, the blades made from the finest of steel, the hilts solid carved ivory.

While all this transpired, a full half dozen Comancheros surrounded Fargo with their weapons drawn. They watched him like hawks, perhaps expecting him to show fear. If so, they were disappointed. Fargo sat with his hands folded in his lap, as composed as he would be if seated in a saloon, playing cards with a bunch of close friends.

Chavez also studied the big man in buckskins and did not seem to like what he saw. He turned to Black Bear as the latter stripped off his buckskin shirt to reveal rippling sinews. "This one does not seem soft like most of his kind, my brother. Maybe we should entertain ourselves another way tonight."

Black Bear gave Fargo a look of utter contempt. "I will carve my name on his belly while he begs for mercy. You should not worry on my account, Caesar."

Fargo saw Jesus go to the middle of the circle and unravel the six-foot sash. When he was done, Armando placed a knife at each end, the hilts facing outward.

The rest of the Comancheros, men and women alike, were gathering just outside the ring of lanterns, encircling the area with a human barrier that would prevent anyone from trying to flee.

Caesar Chavez walked toward Fargo. "It is time, *gringo*. On your feet, please. I am interested to learn if you are as you seem, or whether you are merely a good actor."

Fargo stood. As he did, Belle and Liberty jumped to their feet and stepped in front of him.

"We won't let you do this!" Belle declared.

"You can't stop me, *señorita*," Chavez said with disdain and snapped his fingers. Immediately, five Comancheros seized the sisters, who struggled in vain, and pulled them aside. "If you interfere again," he assured the brunette, "I will have both of your tongues cut out. Comanches do not care for women who talk too much."

Belle was about to give him a piece of her mind, but came to her senses in time.

"Now then," Chavez said, sweeping an arm at the circle with a grand flourish, "after you, *Señor* Fargo. Let us see how easily a *gringo* can bleed."

11

Skye Fargo stood at one end of the red sash. Black Bear stood at the other. Neither paid attention to the murmuring among the encircling Comancheros. Fargo did glance at the sisters, both of whom were terrified, but trying hard not to show it. They regarded him, and rightfully so, as their last chance for salvation, and they feared for his life.

Caesar Chavez strolled around the circle, thumbs hooked in his gunbelt. "How many of us, at one time or another, have listened to a *gringo* brag about his kind?" he asked. "How many of us have been in saloons and heard *gringos* tell how tough they are, and how they can lick their weight in greasers or Comancheros without working up a sweat?"

There was muttering and nods of assent.

"Yet we all know that *gringos* are weaklings," Chavez said smugly. "Take away their guns and they are sniveling cowards. And there is not one who could survive in the Badlands as we do. There is not one who could go as long without water and food as a Comanchero can."

"They are puny!" someone bellowed.

"*Sí,*" Chavez said. "What is worse, they do not know how to die like men. They cry, they whimper, they beg for their lives like children." He pointed at Fargo. "This one will be handed over to the Comanches, and we all know what they will do to him. Let us find out whether he will take it like a man"—he sneered in contempt—"or like the yellow dog he is!"

Fargo listened to some of the Comancheros yip savagely, like a chorus of howling coyotes. Others shouted agreement.

Chavez halted at the edge of the clearing near Juanita, then indicated the sash. "Have you ever been in a sash fight before, *Señor* Fargo?"

"No," Fargo said.

"You pick up your end of the sash and stick it in your mouth. Black Bear will do the same at his end. Then you pick up the Bowie, and on my word, the two of you will fight." Chavez paused. "There are only two rules, *amigo*. You must not let the sash drop from your mouth, and you must not leave the circle."

"And if I do?" Fargo asked.

The leader smirked. "If the sash falls, I will shoot you. Not to kill you, of course, since I want you alive for Little Mountain. But I will put a slug in, oh, your leg or your foot. And you will wish you were dead because it will hurt like hell and we will not doctor you."

"And if I accidentally step from the circle?"

Caesar Chavez looked at the ring of expectant faces, then pulled his knife. Many did likewise. "If you should do that, you will be fair game for those of us watching. I daresay you will be stabbed three or four times before you can get back in, and then only if you are very, very quick." Chavez laughed. "But not to worry, *señor*. We will not stab to kill."

"You're all heart," Fargo said.

"Yes. I always have been too generous for my own good," Chavez joked. "Now, if you please, the sash."

Bending, Fargo raised the material to his mouth and clamped his teeth tight. He thought it was cotton, but that hardly mattered. Black Bear did the same and for several seconds they stood there like two men connected by a single long tongue.

"The Bowies, *por favor*."

Fargo liked the smooth feel of the hilt. He hefted the knife, gauging the balance. The blade shone in the lantern light as he weaved a figure-eight.

Chavez looked at Black Bear. "Remember, I want him alive. Cut him as you please, but do not kill him if you can avoid it. Understand?"

The Comanchero nodded.

"All right," Chavez said, raising both arms for silence. "Begin!"

Fargo crouched, holding the Bowie at chest height, anticipating a cautious probe on the part of his opponent to take the measure of his skill. But Black Bear charged, copperhead quick, slashing deftly, high and low. He was trying to draw blood right away, to get the fight over with swiftly, and he would have succeeded if Fargo had not been as skilled at knife fighting as he was with a pistol and a Sharps.

Ducking and backpedaling, Fargo evaded the initial wicked cut. He parried the next one, their blades ringing like tinny bells, but in so doing snared his arm in the sash, looping it around his wrist. Instantly Black Bear leaped backward, drawing the sash taut and jerking Fargo off balance. Then the Comanchero speared his Bowie inward, confidence glinting in his dagger eyes, going for Fargo's shoulder.

Liberty screamed.

Fargo reacted instinctively. Unable to counter with the Bowie, he twisted while falling forward and threw himself into an agile roll that brought him to his feet beyond Black Bear, unscathed. Quickly he freed his wrist. The Comanchero snarled, feinted, feinted again, then suddenly aimed a vicious blow at Fargo's thigh. Fargo slid his legs wide and the Bowie passed between them. Before Black Bear could recover, Fargo's right arm flashed.

Leaping aside, the Comanchero straightened and touched his fingers to the livid two-inch slit in his cheek. He pressed his tongue to the blood, spat, and bent at the knees, his Bowie close to his waist.

"Get him, Black Bear!" a man cried in encouragement.

"Cut his nose off!" added another.

"Nose, hell! Lop off his balls!" a woman urged.

Which was exactly what Black Bear appeared to have in mind. He thrust at Fargo's groin, but Fargo blocked and glided to the right. Black Bear began bobbing his head, causing the sash to whip up and down.

Fargo promptly realized why. The fluttering sash made it hard for him to keep track of the Comanchero's hands. He tried snapping his head right and left so the sash would swing wide to either side, but it only made the motion of the sash worse. He had no idea where Black Bear's Bowie was. Then he caught a glint of steel as the blade arced at his belly. Fargo wrenched to the left, but was a shade too slow. The razor edge sliced into his buckskin shirt, drawing blood.

Again Black Bear straightened, smiling his scornful smile, his feral eyes saying, "Now we are even, *bastardo*!"

They circled, and Fargo felt the sash slipping. The wetter the cloth became, the harder it was to hold onto. He ground his teeth together and stepped back as far as the sash would allow to give him more room to maneuver.

Black Bear stepped in close, swinging wildly, or so it seemed to Fargo, raining a flurry that drove Fargo rearward. Evading stab after stab, thrust after thrust, Fargo retreated step by step until he heard a sharp intake of breath behind him and abruptly guessed the Comanchero's ploy. Black Bear was trying to force him from the circle.

Fargo sidestepped a lancing blade and glanced over a shoulder. Seven or eight knives waited to drink his blood. He was one step from the edge, one step from being skewered like a piece of meat.

Black Bear darted in closer, sweeping under the sash and driving his knife arm at Fargo's crotch. He thought he had Fargo right where he wanted him, leaving Fargo no choice except to take that final backward step.

Legs coiling like steel springs, Fargo jumped straight up, as high into the air as he could go. Black Bear's blade missed his manhood by inches. For a moment he hung poised above the Comanchero. Then gravity pulled him down, and as he dropped, he snatched at the back of Black Bear's head with his left hand and shoved with all his might.

Black Bear's own momentum worked against him. Arms flailing as he tried to stop, he saw the wall of glittering blades and his mouth slackened. The sash dropped, entangling a leg. Black Bear stumbled, tripped, and smashed headlong into the ranks of fellow Comancheros. It all happened so fast they were caught by surprise. Only a few managed to lower their knives.

A shriek of mortal agony rent the cool night air as Fargo landed in a crouch and spun. He watched Black Bear stagger to the right, futilely trying to stanch a spurting gash in one thigh and a seeping hole on the right side of his chest. And there were other wounds, three or so, bleeding profusely.

Several Comancheros sprang to catch Black Bear as he fell. They lowered him to the grass, trying to hold him still as he writhed in torment.

Fargo rose, lowering his Bowie. An angry murmur broke out, the murmur rapidly becoming a swell of oaths and threats.

A burly Comanchero broke from the line, unlimbering a six-shooter.

"Kill him!" one thundered.

"Shoot him full of lead!"

There was nowhere Fargo could go. Trapped like a wolf at bay, hemmed in on all sides, he glanced right and left as more Comancheros made threatening gestures. It was a matter of seconds before one lost all self-control.

"Enough!" Caesar Chavez roared, striding into the middle of the circle. "I told you he is not to be slain and I meant it!" Rotating, he glared at the ring of furious faces. "Unless there is one of you willing to challenge me, you will do as I say!"

So this was how Comancheros picked their leaders, Fargo mused, staying alert for more trouble. To the toughest went the honor, which he held only so long as he proved faster than anyone who might want to take his place.

Chavez moved to where the stricken Black Bear was being looked after by a pair of women. "Didn't I warn you this Fargo is different? You should have listened. And you should not have been so sure of yourself."

Belle and Liberty Boggs picked that moment to dash over to Fargo. Liberty took his left hand in hers, Belle gave him a hug. When Fargo looked up, Chavez was coming toward them.

"How touching, *señor*," the Comanchero leader said. "The *señoritas* are grateful you were not harmed. But they are grateful too soon." In a blur Chavez drew his pistol. "The ladies will now step back. And you will give your knife to Armando."

Liberty came to Fargo's defense. "Haven't you done enough already? He showed he was better than your man. What more do you want?"

"I want a lot of things, pretty one," Chavez responded. "I want to be filthy rich. I want to leave this godforsaken waste-land and live in a fancy house in a big city. And I want to make love to a different white woman every night." He chuckled. "And if man only had wings, he would fly."

"You're poking fun at me," Liberty said.

"Am I?" Chavez frowned. "*You* would think so, wouldn't you?" His pistol lowered, pointed at Fargo's knee. "Now, *señor*, you will step away from the women and hand over the knife or learn to hobble around on one leg."

Holding his arms out from his sides, Fargo took two strides. Armando, revolver drawn, plucked the knife from his hand and moved off. Loud moans were coming from Black Bear, who was slick with blood from chest to ankles.

"Take the women to the shack," Chavez ordered. A half dozen Comancheros moved to obey. When the sisters tried to resist, they were cuffed across the face and shoved from the circle.

Fargo had a gut feeling that something awful was about to take place. He saw Chavez holster the pistol, saw other Comancheros moving in to surround him. And if looks could kill, he'd be a pulped mass of skin and bones.

"I am very disappointed in how the sash fight turned out," Caesar Chavez commented. "Since I was the one who suggested it, I am partly to blame for the pain Black Bear is suffering, pain you were supposed to suffer."

Fargo suspected that any reply he made might be taken as an excuse to tear into him so he stayed silent. Not that it did him any good.

"Pain is remarkable, is it not?" Chavez had gone on. "There are so many kinds. Some only bother us a little, like a toothache. Some, like that which Black Bear feels, make us wish we were dead." He folded his arms. "Some of us hold up well under pain. Some do not. Which are you?"

The Comancheros who had surrounded Fargo replaced their six-shooters and knives. A number of them smacked clenched fists into open palms. Others cracked their knuckles or laughed.

Fargo slowly turned, seeking a weak link in the chain. But every one of them had that tough-as-nails look of the hardened killer. They would not give an inch. Nor would they show him the slightest mercy.

Caesar Chavez did not mince words. He simply said, "Do it," and stepped to one side.

In a concerted rush the Comancheros converged. Fargo brought his fists up to defend himself, but he only deflected one punch when a human hailstorm plowed into him with knuckles flying, and it felt as if he was being punched everywhere at once. Blows struck his head, his back, his front. He buckled under the fierce attack, falling to his knees with his arms raised to cover his face. But his arms were grabbed and pulled aside, and a ringing right cross nailed him flush on the jaw.

Fargo swallowed blood, spied a groin in front of him, and rammed a left into the Comanchero. The man screeched, tottered away. Two more instantly took his place, beating Fargo on the head and shoulders.

Through a swirling daze of popping light Fargo realized they were holding back, using only enough force to bruise him, not enough to break bones or kill. It was small consolation. Pain seemed to fill every pore in his body. A fist clipped his cheek, crunching his teeth together. Sheer rage lent him the strength to drop two Comancheros. Punching like a madman, he gained his feet.

"What is the matter with you?" Chavez snarled at his men. "He is only one man!"

Stung by the rebuke, the Comancheros redoubled their assault. Fargo ducked under a jab to the nose and was hit on the left temple. Staggered, he buried his right fist in the stomach of the man responsible and was struck four times by four different Comancheros. One of them pounded him low on the back, sending a wave of agony up his spine. Involuntarily, he arched his back, his arms dropping, and like a pack of wolves tearing at a helpless elk the Comancheros swarmed over him. Fargo dimly felt his jaw take a series of punishing blows. Then the stars faded, the lanterns died, and the ground swept up to meet him.

After a while Fargo thought he heard voices. He thought he was being carried by rough, callused hands. His consciousness swam, flickered, and was lost.

It was the cool feel of a wet cloth on his brow that brought Fargo around once more. He felt sluggish, woozy, as if his blood pumped through his veins in slow motion. He didn't open his eyes right away, but lay there combating the cocoon of pain sheathing his body, pain so intense he wanted to scream. He suppressed the urge, though, refusing to give the Comancheros the satisfaction.

A soft hand tenderly touched Fargo's lips. Expecting to see Belle, he opened his eyes. Liberty sat next to him, downcast. She gave a start, then grinned in relief.

"Goodness, you scared me! I didn't think you'd revive until tonight sometime."

"Where . . . ?" Fargo began, trying to sit up. The pain had other ideas and it won.

"Where are you? In the same filthy hole they've kept us in since we got here," Liberty said.

Over her shoulder Belle appeared. "I don't need to ask how you are. I've never seen anyone with so many black and blue marks in all my life."

"Thanks," Fargo muttered, grunting as he propped a hand on the dirt floor and tried once more to sit. He succeeded, but a solid iron hammer of pure pain pounded the inside of his skull. "You sure know how to cheer a man up." Twisting his head, he saw sunlight framed in the window. Just outside the entrance sat a stolid Comanchero, rifle in his lap. "How long was I out?"

"All night and half the morning," Liberty said. "We tried to bring you around sooner, but they'd beat on your noggin something terrible."

"Believe me. I know." Fargo placed his other hand flat and pushed. His legs wanted to cooperate, but the pain wouldn't let them.

"Don't exert yourself so much yet," Belle said. "Give it time."

"Time is one thing we can't afford to waste," Fargo said. "We have to figure a way out of this fix before the Comanches show up."

Liberty wrung her hands in her lap. "That could be at any time," she commented. "Chavez came by at dawn. He's real upset with you."

"Black Bear died," Belle explained. "Bled to death. Nothing they did helped."

"Couldn't have happened to a nicer *hombre*," Fargo joked. Gingerly, he felt along his jaw. Everywhere he touched, no matter how lightly, provoked exquisite pangs. He looked down at himself. His shirt had been torn, exposing skin more blue than white. The stab wound had congealed. Only two inches long, it was the very least of his worries.

"I thought for sure you were a goner when that Comanchero tried to stab you," Liberty said.

"Was that why you screamed?"

The blonde shaded pink and turned her face away. "There's no denying I like you. We both do. If the death of our pa wasn't sitting so heavy on my heart, I'd be in a better frame of mind to show you exactly how much."

Fargo suddenly realized they had no idea Phinneas lived. "Your father isn't dead," he stated. "We found him in time."

Both women brightened and clutched him in a tizzy of excitement. "Alive? You're sure?" Liberty asked. Belle threw in, "How bad off was he? We had to sit and watch helplessly, tied to our saddles, as that son of a bitch Baxter beat on him with a six-gun. Pa wasn't moving when we rode off."

"He's in a bad way," Fargo admitted, "but he was able to talk and move a little." He placed a hand on each of them and tenderly squeezed. "Don't worry. Phinneas has a strong constitution. He'll pull through."

"He won't need no sawbones, either," Belle said. "His patent medicines will put him on his feet in no time."

"You really believe that, don't you?"

"Of course I do." Belle squatted. "Pa told us about the talk the two of you had in the wagon. You think he's a fake, don't you?"

"Let's just say I've had my doubts and let it go at that," Fargo answered.

Two luscious mouths curved downward.

"You saw with your own eyes how much care Pa takes with his medicines," Liberty defended her father. "Would a flim-flam man go to the lengths he does to ensure his ingredients are mixed properly? Or offer folks their money back if the cures don't work?"

"I'd be the first to agree there are a lot of confidence men posing as legitimate patent medicine men," Belle chimed in, "but our pa isn't one of them. He tests all his new concoctions, giving them away free to people who need different cures. And if the medicines don't work, he throws them out and starts all over again."

"A cold cure and pimple remover combined?" Fargo said skeptically.

"It works. I swear," Belle said. "I still remember when he invented it. I was only ten. He wanted something that would ease the effects of colds, and since I had one at the time, he used it on me. Made me sick as a dog for a day, then I was good as new. No sign of that old cold."

Liberty nodded. "And I was the one who discovered it

would remove pimples. I liked to rub it on my cheeks because the alcohol in the medicine made my skin all tingly and the rose scent was so sweet. Well, darn it if didn't take away all the pimples I had back then."

They were so earnest that Fargo didn't have the heart to tell them he still didn't believe their father's medicines could cure as well as they claimed. He was spared being quizzed on the matter by a commotion outside.

"What's all the yelling about?" Liberty asked, rising. She went to the window, then reported, "All the Comancheros are gathering in the big clearing. And the women are making for the tents and lean-tos like their dresses are on fire."

"I want to see for myself," Fargo said. He tried to stand and got halfway up before the room spun madly and he started to pitch forward.

Belle caught him, lowered him to his hands and knees. "I warned you not to exert yourself. Whatever is happening out there doesn't concern us. You need to lie down and catch up on your rest."

"No," Fargo said. He girded his muscles, planted his feet firmly, and shot erect before the dizziness could assail him. A single wobbly stride was all he took when the doorway changed places with the roof and both hopped like jackrabbits. He thought he was going to be sick. Holding a hand to his forehead, he shuffled to the entrance and leaned on the edge of the right-hand plank.

"Stubborn as a mule," Belle groused.

Fargo was too interested in the Comancheros to respond. They faced in the direction of the mouth of the canyon, and there, billowing on the hot wind, rose a large column of dust. "You were wrong," he told Belle.

"About what? You being stubborn?"

"About whatever is happening not concerning us. It does."

Fargo sagged, thinking they had gone from the frying pan into the fire. "That dust means the Comanches have arrived."

12

Little Mountain was aptly named. Towering shy of seven feet high and having the bulk of a grizzly, he made the war horse he rode seem puny by comparison. He wore his long hair loose except for a single thin braid adorned by a lone feather. His bare barrel chest was crisscrossed with bandoliers filled with cartridges for the old Sharps he carried.

"Oh, God," Liberty said, observing the giant dismount in front of Caesar Chavez. "I'd rather die than let that brute slobber all over me."

Fargo was counting the Comanches. There were fourteen, including Little Mountain. Added to the Comancheros, he was up against a small army. And in his condition he couldn't whip a scrappy ten-year-old.

"Will they come for us right away?" Belle inquired.

"They'll palaver a while, swap lies about how tough they are, how many men they've killed," Fargo said. "Chavez won't send for us until the Comanches have ate and drank their fill. He'll try to get Little Mountain drunk so he can get the better of the deal when they dicker over how much the two of you are worth."

"I hope they choke on their food," Liberty said.

Fargo tried to catch sight of the sun, but the door and window opened to the west. By the size of the shadows, he figured it was somewhere between ten and eleven in the morning. Far too early. Everything depended on how long the palaver took. Unless it ran until dark, their goose, as the old saw went, was cooked. He stepped to a corner and sank down, fatigue dragging at him like an anvil around his neck.

Liberty looked at Belle, who nodded, then sidled over and sat so her shoulder brushed his. "I'm sorry there's nothing we can do for you, especially after everything you've done on our behalf."

"Save your thanks for when we get out of here," Fargo said.

"Why'd you come after us, anyhow? We figured you were too mad at Pa to give a damn."

Leaning back, Fargo closed his eyes and sighed. "Do you really need to ask?"

"No, I suppose not. But I hate to think that you might die on our account."

"That makes two of us."

Liberty snuggled against him, laying her head on his upper arm. "Get us out of this fix, and I'll make it well worth your while," she whispered.

"Belle won't mind?"

"We're sisters. We learned a long time ago to share and share alike." Liberty grinned. "Although we do bicker like spatting cats over who has the right to share first."

Fargo opened his eyes and rubbed them to keep from falling asleep. As he dropped his arm, Liberty looked up coyly, giggled like a little girl about to have her first kiss, and did just that, molding her lips to his before he quite realized her intent. His mouth, so puffy and tender, pulsed with a smarting sensation that made him want to cringe. He held out, responding as best he could, counting on her to end it soon.

Evidently in no hurry, Liberty rested her palms on his shoulders and began to mash her mouth into his.

"Whoa there!" Fargo said, prying her loose. "There's a time and a place for everything and this isn't it for that."

"Spoilsport," Liberty griped, but she sat back and flattened the wrinkles in her dress. "I'll take you at your word."

The next several hours were an ordeal of heat, thirst, hunger, and dirt. Fargo dozed, waking every so often to peer out at the Comancheros and Comanches. Bottles were being passed around, and there was much loud talk and laughter. Despite the friendly appearances, he knew there lurked an underlying tension. The Comanches sat by themselves behind their chief, while the Comancheros kept weapons within swift reach. The two sides were trading partners, but they had yet to learn to trust one another.

Chavez kept a bottle in front of Little Mountain at all times. Fargo noticed the warrior polish one off and act a little tipsy, but he suspected the chief's capacity for liquor was much higher than Little Mountain let on. Two could play at Chavez's game.

At noon the cooking fires were stoked and pots hung out. The women prepared stew, tossing in the meat of a few rabbits, lizards, and snakes. Its aromatic scent carried to the shack, giving Fargo's stomach fits.

"I'd eat a sidewinder's rattles long about now," Liberty said.

Belle went to the door. "How about us? Do we eat, too?"

"Why should you?" the guard rejoined without deigning to turn. "Are you Comancheros?" He found his humor tremendously funny and guffawed long and loud.

"We won't be any use to you if we starve," Belle said.

"Missing a meal won't hurt you, bitch. Women are like horses. The more you overfeed them, the more cantankerous they become." The guard sniggered. "That's why Comanches like their horses and their women skinny."

Defeated, Belle plopped onto the dirt floor beside Fargo. "I've never felt so helpless," she confided. "If not for you being here, I would have given up long ago."

"Me too," Liberty said.

"We're not licked yet," Fargo assured them, but that was all he would say in case the guard's ears were as sharp as his tongue. Several more hours trickled past. The laughter outside lessened, and when next Fargo looked out, Chavez and Little Mountain were having a heated discussion. "It won't be long now," he forewarned the sisters. And sunset was hours away.

"You seem to have a handle on how these vermin work," Belle said. "What will happen next?"

"Chavez will send for you so Little Mountain can examine the goods. The Comanche will fondle every inch of your bodies, then complain you're not fit to mend his moccasins, in order to drive the price down. Chavez will say you're the finest beauties he's ever laid eyes on and demand top dollar. And when Little Mountain balks, Chavez will have me brought out and offer to throw me in as a bonus if Little Mountain will meet his price. Since Comanches love torturing whites almost as much as they do crawling under a buffalo robe with a white woman, they'll clinch the deal."

Liberty balled her hands in anger. "Isn't there anything we can do?"

Fargo glanced at the guard, who was watching the proceedings, then quickly hunkered down in front of the women and whispered, "I wanted to wait for nightfall, but now we can't. Do both of you know where the horses are tied?"

"Around behind this shack and down the knoll," Belle said. "But what good does that do us? We'll be caught before we can reach them."

"Maybe not," Fargo said, peeling his pants above his boots. From his right boot he drew the Arkansas toothpick, from the left a little insurance he had bought in Rawbone in case he tangled with Cull Holman's outfit along the trail. Since they'd known about his knife, he'd purchased a Colt .32-caliber pocket pistol to use as a last resort if the old man didn't keep his word and tried to lynch Phinneas without benefit of a trial. As things had turned out, the hideout proved unnecessary. Until now.

"You've had them all this time?" Liberty said in astonishment. "Why didn't you use them sooner?"

"And be shot on the spot?" Fargo said. Standing, he whispered, "Stand up and go to the right of the door." Then he stepped to the doorway, his arms close to his sides, the weapons hidden behind his legs. The guard glanced sharply at him as he casually leaned against the jamb. "You've made it plain we can't have any food," he said good-naturedly. "But how about some more water?"

"You'll drink when we say you drink, *gringo,* and not before," snapped the Comanchero. "Get back in there. And all three of you stop pestering me. You're worse than flies."

Fargo nodded. "Whatever you say. I don't want any more trouble than I already have."

"You're smart for a white man." The guard chuckled and resumed watching the talk.

Shifting, Fargo made as if to obey. His eyes flicked toward the Comanches and Comancheros; as near as he could tell, no one was looking at the shack. Spinning, he reached the guard in one step and jammed the barrel of the pocket pistol against the man's head while cocking the piece. "Do anything and you die."

126

The half-breed stiffened and foolishly began to lift his rifle, but caught himself in time and froze.

"You're smart for a Comanchero," Fargo said. "Now I want you to stand up and back into the shack. Make no sudden moves, and don't yell out or else." The man stood and Fargo slipped behind him, jabbing the toothpick into his spine for added incentive. Together they retreated into the hovel. "Hand your rifle to the *señorita* with dark hair."

Belle took it.

Fargo whipped the pistol on high, then slammed it into the man's temple. The small revolver lacked heft, but was heavy enough to cause the Comanchero to totter. He opened his mouth to shout as Fargo slugged him a second time, dropping him in the dirt.

Fargo glanced at the sisters. "When we go out the door, make straight for the string. Whatever you do, don't stop. Once you're on a horse, head for the gap."

Both nodded grimly. Liberty was waxen.

"Let's hope they don't spot us until it's too late," Fargo said. At the doorway he surveyed the camp. Chavez was handing a rifle to Little Mountain, the chief grinning like a kid given a new toy. Fargo felt a twinge of anger on recognizing the gun. It was his Sharps, but there was nothing he could do about it. Most of the Comancheros appeared bored, the Comanches listless.

"Now," Fargo whispered and dashed to the corner. Pausing, he let the women go by so he could cover them. As yet there had not been any outcry. They hastened past a tent and several lean-tos and were almost to the horses when a Comanchero woman came around a tree in front of them, a bundle of firewood in her arms. She instantly threw back her head and screeched.

Belle silenced her by slamming the rifle into her jaw. The woman crumpled, and Belle and Liberty raced the final few yards.

Fargo followed, backpedaling. He heard alarmed shouts, saw men leaping to their feet. Passing the women, who had mounted, he reached the Ovaro and untied the reins. He regretted having to leave his saddle and bedroll, but they could be replaced. His life couldn't. Gripping the stallion's mane, he swung on and joined the sisters, who had dallied despite his instructions. "What the hell are you waiting for?" he asked.

"You," Liberty said.

"Ride!" Fargo commanded, giving her horse a slap on the rump. Side by side the sisters galloped off. He looked back, found Comancheros and Comanches spilling around both ends of the shack. He'd wanted to stampede the rest of the horses, but lingering meant certain death. Snapping a shot at the on-rushing pack of killers to slow them down, he wheeled and fled, expecting a crackle of gunfire to speed them on their way.

No gunshots sounded. Fargo thought that strange until he realized Chavez and Little Mountain would want the women alive. For that matter, they'd want him alive, too, so they could torture him at their leisure.

The fleetest of the Comancheros were already to the string and were scrambling to mount skittish animals.

Fargo brought the pinto to a gallop, rapidly overtaking the women. Belle rode easily, at home in the saddle. Liberty tried hard, but she was less experienced. Fargo came alongside her and raised his voice to be heard above the drumming of hooves. "When we reach the gap, go on through and keep on going. Head due north."

"What about you?"

"I'll try to slow down our friends."

"We can help."

"Do as you're told," Fargo said sternly. He'd have enough on his hands without having to worry about them also. So far they were maintaining their lead over the few Comancheros already chasing them, but that might change.

The flat, open land worked in their favor. Presently the canyon entrance materialized, and once again Fargo slowed so the sisters could go first. They filed into the gap at a trot. The foremost Comancheros were now in rifle range, but Belle had the rifle. Fargo raised the pocket pistol, thinking another shot might discourage them, then changed his mind. He should conserve his bullets for the time he really needed them.

Getting through the gap seemed to take forever. The narrow walls and constant bends forced them to walk their mounts. Fargo sought sign of boulders perched on the rim which he might be able to dislodge with well-placed shots, blocking the passage, but there were none.

Eventually, Belle gave a cry of joy, and they emerged from stony confinement into the harsh glare of the late afternoon sun. The sisters pressed on, Liberty scowling at being separated.

Fargo listened and heard, deep in the recesses of the notch, the faint clatter of hooves. Moving to the left, he held the pocket Colt in his hand and waited. The figures of the sisters diminished in size, becoming stick silhouettes by the time the loud crack of a hoof on stone told Fargo the first Comanchero was about to emerge. Muffled voices could be heard. He guessed they were debating whether it was safe to come on out.

It wasn't. Fargo spurred the Ovaro to the opening. Ten feet away sat Armando, twisted sideways in the saddle, speaking to the man behind him. Armando saw Fargo, cursed, and grabbed for his six-shooter. Fargo was quicker, putting a shot into the Comanchero's right eye and two more into Armando's horse. The animal floundered, sagged forward, and pitched onto its chest, spilling Armando over its neck. Oaths and bellows broke out from those behind. Pistols spat lead and smoke.

Fargo was in motion before Armando's mount fell. He disliked killing the horse, but it had to be done. By plugging the opening he'd bought a little time. It would take an hour or more for the Comancheros to move the obstacle. By then he'd be well away.

The Ovaro galloped across the baking Badlands with mane and tail flying. Fargo wedged the small Colt under his belt to free his hands for the business of riding a long distance. Tiny specks on the horizon guided him toward the sisters.

Skye Fargo was no fool. He knew the reprieve would be short-lived, and that the Comancheros would be as mad as a swarm of riled hornets when they managed to clear the gap. Alone, he'd have no problem outrunning them. With the women along, he had to either come up with a brainstorm to shake the Comancheros or find a spot to make a desperate stand.

The searing heat was almost unbearable. Fargo and the Ovaro were soon perspiring heavily, and he made a mental note that if he lived, he was never, ever going to enter the Badlands again unless his life depended on it. Even then he'd think twice.

The specks grew larger much more swiftly than they should have. Fargo frowned, suspecting why, his suspicion verified when he drew within three hundred yards of the sisters and could see they were walking their mounts instead of riding hard. They saw him, reined up, and Liberty waved.

"Do you have rocks for brains?" Fargo said as he caught up. "Or do you *want* to spend the rest of your days being at Little Mountain's beck and call?"

"We couldn't up and desert you," Liberty said.

Fargo gripped her arm, his fingers digging into her creamy skin. "When I tell you to do something, do it. You should have been five miles farther by now, fives miles we can't make up."

"You're hurting me!" Liberty protested, striving to free herself.

"It's nothing compared to what Little Mountain will do to you," Fargo declared.

"Go easy on her, Skye," Belle said. "She was just concerned, is all. I told her it wouldn't hurt to slow down some."

Fargo turned on her. "You were wrong. And I figured you, at least, would know better." He scanned the wasteland to the south and spied a mushroom shaped puff of dust at the limits of his vision. "Now we'll be lucky if we can stay ahead of them until dark." Flicking his reins, he barked, "Let's ride."

There was a grotesque sameness about the Badlands. The farther a person went, the more the landscape blurred into a monotonous duplication of itself. It gave Fargo the impression of riding mile after mile and not really getting anywhere.

The mushroom cloud expanded, but not drastically. Fargo estimated their pursuers were seven or eight miles behind. He wanted to get past the stretch of cliffs and gorges to the flatland before dark, but the women had lost too much ground to accomplish that.

Fargo reckoned they were a mile or two shy of the flatland when the sun sank. He was disappointed, since they could have ridden on through the night with little fear of a spill. But there was a ray of hope; the Comanches and Comancheros hadn't overtaken them.

A gorge offered a safe haven. Fargo dismounted, took the rifle from Belle, and hiked half a mile along their back trail. Crouched at the base of a leaning spiral of rock, he bided his time until convinced the Comancheros weren't coming.

A small fire crackled in the gorge, carefully hidden at the base of a rock wall. The sisters were huddled together, talking softly in worried tones. They each gasped when he loomed out of the gloom.

"Damn, Skye! Scare a woman to death, why don't you?" Belle said.

"Sorry." Fargo squatted. "It looks as if we're safe until morning, but I'll stand guard just the same."

"We'll all take turns," Liberty amended. "Or have you forgotten that us Boggs's hold our own?"

"No, I'll never take a Boggs lightly again," Fargo promised wryly, sitting so he faced the gorge mouth. "Who started the fire?"

"Me," Belle responded. "Took forever rubbing two sticks together." She paused. "I hope you don't mind. We don't need the heat, but the light helps lighten the spirits. And I put it where no one could see it."

"You did fine," Fargo said. He rested against the wall, his battered body craving sleep he could ill afford to take. "I'll keep watch first. Then Liberty. Then Belle." A low whinny reminded him of something else. "And I'll give the horses a rubdown."

Rising wearily, Fargo moved beyond the firelight where the three horses stood with heads hanging. Of them, the Ovaro was in the best shape. He hoped the others wouldn't falter tomorrow. Their lives hung in the balance.

He searched and found clumps of dry grass. Taking a handful, he gave the pinto a thorough rubdown, then started on the second animal. Engrossed in the task, resisting the fatigue that ate at him, he nearly missed hearing the scrape of a foot on gravel.

The rifle was propped on a nearby boulder. Fargo resorted to the Colt pocket pistol, clearing his belt and whirling, seeking the outline of the Comanchero or Comanche stalking him.

Instead, he saw Liberty, her blond hair cascading over her shoulders. "Trying to get yourself killed?"

"I came to help."

"Don't need any," Fargo said. He continued rubbing and heard her come up behind him.

"And I wanted to talk."

"About what?"

"You."

Fargo didn't stop working.

Liberty cleared her throat. "You've been awful hard on us today, particularly me. And all because I've been worried about you. The way you've been snapping at us, a body would think you didn't care about our feelings one whit."

There it was. Plainly stated. Fargo grinned despite himself and bent to stroke low down.

"I suppose I shouldn't blame you," Liberty went on. "We've all had a lot on our minds, and anyone would be a mite cranky after being beaten with an inch of their lives."

"You done?"

"Not yet. I just wanted you to know you don't have to carry the whole weight of this thing on your shoulders alone. Belle and I will do our part to help."

Straightening, Fargo rested his forearms on the sorrel. "You've already made that clear. Why don't you run along and get some sleep while you can?"

"I have more to say."

"Could have fooled me." Fargo walked to the last horse, and she dogged his heels.

"It's not enough that you treat us as if we're girls instead of grown women," Liberty lectured him. "But you never notice when someone is trying to favor you with the kind of interest most men would die for. Why, a woman must have to hit you over the head with a mallet before she can get your attention."

Sighing, Fargo looked at the crumpled grass in his hand, then tossed it aside and faced her. Women always picked the damnedest times, he reflected. But they should be all right so long as the Comancheros had in fact halted for the night. Liberty was babbling on about some men having heads like marble. "Why don't you quit flapping your gums," he told her, "and do what you came here to do."

"You smug bastard," the blonde said, smiling. "You saw right through me." Her eyes sparkling with inner lust, she sashayed up to him and pressed her lush form into his. "How ever did you know?"

13

It never ceased to amaze Fargo how women could go through grueling ordeals that left men reeking like a swamp and come out smelling like a rose. The long ride was a perfect illustration. He was sweaty, grimy, badly in need of a bath. Yet Liberty was as fresh and spotless as if she'd merely taken a short stroll, her hair smelling of smoke, her skin as aromatic as a bouquet of roses. He knew she must have cleaned herself up while he was gone, but he couldn't imagine how she had done it.

Now, enfolding her in his arms, Fargo paused to inhale and peck her on the neck. "It never occurred to you to wait until we reach Rawbone?"

"Who are you trying to fool? We might never see Rawbone again." Liberty put her hands on his chest. "And I want something to remember life by."

Her inviting lips, parted like the delicate petals of a flower, drew Fargo's mouth like a magnet. He kissed her softly, his tongue dancing with hers. She ran her hands down his back to his buttocks and cupped them.

Belle had been delightful in her own right, but Liberty showed early on that she was all any man ever asked of a woman. She was the more aggressive of the two, and as many a man before Fargo had learned, aggressive women were better lovers. Making love to a wildcat was always more enjoyable than making love to a bump on a log.

So Fargo didn't mind when her nails raked his lower back. He tingled when she ran a hand around his leg to his groin and rubbed his swelling manhood. And he felt his blood pump wildly when she slipped that same hand under his belt and down his pants.

"You don't beat around the bush," he said when they broke to breathe.

"Never have," Liberty said. "I may not shoot like Belle or ride like Belle, but when it comes to men I'm the one who drains them dry and leaves them panting for more."

Fargo smirked. "Prove it."

Liberty did her best. Her mouth roved his face and throat, her hand roved his pole, while her body wriggled enticingly against his to arouse him further. He undid the top of her dress, then hiked the hem high to stroke her superb thighs. He was taken aback when his knuckles brushed between her legs and there was no underwear.

Cupping her bottom, Fargo bodily picked her up and moved past the third horse to a sheltered nook. Her long legs wrapped around his hips. He backed her into a corner and plunged a hand inside her dress to squeeze her breasts.

"I knew you'd be good!" Liberty husked.

Fargo rimmed her nether lips with his finger. She cooed, then bit him on the shoulder. He hardly noticed. His mouth, his cheeks, his chest were already in pain, but he shut it from his mind and concentrated on the pleasure. Her right hand was doing things to his manhood the likes of which no one had done in ages.

"My big, wonderful stallion," she said in his ear.

His mouth descended to her breasts. The nipples were nails, her skin as supple as the softest leather. He hungrily inhaled them, his tongue squiggling back and forth.

Liberty played with his ear, rubbed the nape of his neck, and lifted her leg so her knee pressed on his throbbing organ. Her hot breath fanned his forehead.

Fargo switched from her right breast to her left. His fingers stroked her slit, provoking a throaty growl of sensual satisfaction. Then he shoved a finger into her, and she jumped as if swatted. Her slick inner walls closed on his finger like a silken glove.

"Priming the pump, sugar?"

Two fingers brought a hiss of air from her lungs. Liberty lifted his head to plant her damp lips on his. She sucked his tongue into her mouth, swirling it around and around. Every time he pumped his fingers, she sucked. The sensation sent goose bumps rippling down his back.

135

Fargo reached down to free his organ and discovered she had rendered the service for him. He touched the tip to her core and she quivered in anticipation.

"Put it in. All the way in."

"Not quite yet." Fargo slowly removed his fingers and used them to pinch a nipple. She took the hand in hers, raised the fingers to her mouth, and sucked on them while grinding her hips into his. Her eyes glowed with passion, her expression yearning for physical release.

Fargo held her buttocks in both hands and applied pressure on her thighs with his thumbs. She willingly parted her legs to accommodate him.

"Now?" Liberty asked.

"Now," Fargo said, and impaled her.

"Ohhhhhhhhhh, myyyyyyy!"

A pulse pounding current of ecstasy brought Fargo to his toes. He drove into her like a human piston. Her back was braced by the wall behind her, her weight borne by his waist and hands. She stuck her tongue between her lips and blew through her nose, head tossing from side to side.

Fargo paced himself, listening to the slap of their muscled stomachs. He fastened his mouth on her right breast, a hand on the other. She tried to get him to go faster by wriggling her bottom suggestively, but he refused to do as she wanted.

He had forgotten all about listening for footfalls or hoof-beats. So when a noise he couldn't explain intruded on his bliss, he was all the more concerned. Glancing back, he saw one of the horses poking at grass with a front hoof.

"Don't stop, lover!" Liberty coaxed. "Please don't stop!"

Fargo put his hands under her arms for better leverage, then rammed into her with practiced skill. She trembled, clawed his arms, panting heavily. The grip of her smooth sheath tightened of its own accord.

"Oh, Skye! I think . . ." Liberty started to exclaim, and moaned as her nether regions gushed.

Until now Fargo had held himself back. The feeling of her spurting over him was the trigger that shot him over the edge. Venting a guttural snarl, he crested, a million fireworks bursting before his eyes. He emptied himself in hard, long thrusts. When he was done, they sagged against one another, totally spent.

"We should have done that sooner," Liberty lamented.

"Don't blame me. I was waiting for you to pay me a visit."

Fargo slid out of her and lowered her to the ground. She nibbled on his chin, licked his nose.

"If we make it to Rawbone, you'll have to put a lock on your door to keep me out of your room."

The wind had increased during their lovemaking. It brought to Fargo's ears the distant wail of a coyote, the first he'd heard since entering the Badlands. Or was it a coyote? he mused. Could it be a Comanche tracking them down? Comanches were said to be nearly as skilled as Apaches.

"Something wrong?" Liberty had sensed the change in him.

"Probably not," Fargo answered, "but it might be best if we rejoined your sister."

Belle was still by her small fire, her eyes hooded as if she were dozing. Something in her face, the way the corners of her mouth crinkled slightly, told Fargo she was wide awake and had been listening the whole time. He pretended to be fooled, and after Liberty sat, he hefted the rifle and moved into the shadows beyond the fire, saying over his shoulder, "I'll wake you when it's your turn."

His watch went well. The howl wasn't repeated. Nor did he hear anything else out of the ordinary. He had to shake Liberty several times before she sluggishly sat up.

"So soon?"

"Afraid so." Fargo gave her the rifle. "Use this only if you have to. And don't fall asleep or—"

"—or you'll paddle my fanny?" she asked hopefully.

"Wishful thinking." Fargo sank down near Belle. Through sheer force of will he had held his exhaustion at bay. Now he succumbed, sinking into a black, bottomless well. It seemed as if he had just closed his eyes when he was being urgently shaken and a tense voice was saying his name over and over.

"Skye! Skye! Oh, please wake up! They're coming!"

Fargo blinked, the panic on Belle's face hitting him like a blow to the solar plexus. The sky was still dark, filled with stars. Since the fire had long since gone out, he could barely make out her features. "So soon? It's not dawn yet."

"I know." Belle motioned southward. "Give a listen. Tell me if my imagination got the best of me."

Fargo was so worn out he had to rely on the wall behind

him for support as he stood. He stretched, then yawned. Liberty was curled into a ball close by, angelic in repose.

"Listen!" Belle breathed.

"I don't hear anything," Fargo said, taking a few steps. There was the wind, the rustle of patches of dry grass, and Liberty's snoring. About to turn, he heard, clear and unmistakable on the rarified air, the faint creak of saddle leather. "Damn."

"Was I right? Is it them?"

"It's not the Pony Express. You wake your sister. I'll fetch the horses."

By the positions of the constellations Fargo figured it was an hour until first light. The wily Comancheros were counting on them to be so bushed they'd sleep until sunrise and find themselves surrounded. Thanks to Belle, the sons of bitches were going to have their day ruined.

Liberty was wide awake and raring to go. She winked slyly at Skye as she mounted, giving him a flash of her thigh.

The damnedest times, Fargo mentally repeated as he climbed onto the stallion. "We head due north," he reminded the women. "Provided the horses hold out, we should be quit of the Badlands by dark or shortly after."

"I, for one, can hardly wait to stop again," Liberty said.

Fargo shook his head and spurred the stallion into a trot. From the gorge he wound along a short cliff, avoided a ravine, and as the blazing glory of the rising sun crowned the world with its glaring brilliance, he reached the alkaline flats.

By seven the temperature was at seventy. By nine, at ninety. By half past ten or so, pushing a hundred.

The horses performed well, although Belle's gave Fargo cause to fret. Every so often it favored its left foreleg. He stopped once to examine the limb and found nothing wrong. By the middle of the afternoon the animals were plodding across the bleak terrain, heads bowed, shoulders slumped.

Belle licked her chapped lips. "Do you think we've lost them?"

"I doubt they'll give up shy of Rawbone," Fargo predicted.

"They want us that bad?"

"They want the two of you that bad. I'm sort of the frosting on the cake."

Liberty laughed. "Sweet-tasting frosting, too."

From the ridge where Fargo had spent his first night in the Badlands they scanned the country they had covered and spotted the dust cloud they dreaded would be there.

"Five miles?" Liberty said.

"More like ten," Fargo responded.

"It's not enough," Belle remarked.

Once the sun slipped toward the west, and the temperature began to drop, the horses regained enough stamina to hold to a trot. Islands of grass broke the stranglehold of the alkaline. Then the grassland itself was in front of them, and even though the horses were famished, Fargo pushed ever northward. There would be time enough for the animals to graze once they had lost themselves in the rolling woodland. Twilight had come and was nearly gone when Fargo beheld a line of trees to the northwest.

"We made it!" Liberty yelled.

"Not yet," Fargo said.

The welcome coolness of the forest closed around them with refreshing suddenness. Fargo rode for another hour, until even the pinto flagged. In a clearing lush with grass he stopped. Removing the bridle, he turned the Ovaro loose to graze and shambled under an oak tree.

Liberty had her hand pressed to the small of her back as she walked stiffly over. "Lord, I ache from head to toe. I think I died and no one bothered to tell me."

"Will we keep watch again tonight?" Belle inquired.

"Of course," Fargo said. "And no fire. We don't know how close they are, and we can't risk them seeing it." The rifle in the crook of his arm, he walked the border of the clearing, paying special attention to their back trail. A small part of him wanted to believe the Comancheros had given up. But he knew better.

It gave him the ideal excuse to put Liberty off. Fargo figured the sex-starved blonde would want to go into the brush and rip his pants down, and he didn't care to confess he was simply too tired. So as he neared the oak tree, he was all set to explain about the Comancheros. Only there was no need. The sisters were lying back to back, both in slumberland.

Moving off so as not to disturb them, Fargo paced to keep from becoming drowsy. The drone of crickets lent weight to his fatigue, lulling him into thinking all was well. He halted and leaned on the rifle, his eyelids feeling truly like marble.

What woke him, Fargo couldn't say. He knew he'd fallen asleep standing up, and he was annoyed at his lapse. Suddenly, he realized the crickets were silent. And in the woods to the south a horse nickered.

Fargo sped to the women and shook each in turn. "Get up. We have to ride." They sat up slowly, their bodies moving as if they were thawing out from being frozen.

"What did you say?" Belle asked, slurring the words.

"The Comancheros are almost on us."

That did the trick. In very short order Fargo was leading them out of the clearing. Another whinny, this time much, much closer, revealed how narrow their escape had been. Imminent danger crackled in the air itself.

Fargo held the horses to a walk, reining up frequently to listen. He sensed rather than heard many Comancheros in the forest and figured they were closing in on the clearing. Touching a finger to his lips, he rode due west, sticking to tracts where there was less brush.

Any sound at all might give them away—the squeak of a saddle, the clop of a hoof, the swish of a tail against a limb.

The next time Fargo halted, he passed the Colt pocket pistol to Belle and the toothpick to Liberty. They needed to be able to defend themselves should their flight be cut short. He was lifting the reins when a huge shadow detached itself from a tree on the right and charged them.

Automatically, Fargo took a bead, then fired. The rider let out a squawk as he toppled. On all sides shouts split the night. Undergrowth cracked and splintered as Comancheros tore through the woods toward them.

"Ride!" Fargo cried, galloping past the thrashing form of the one he'd shot. Somewhere a gun boomed and was punctuated by a yell from Caesar Chavez.

"No firing, *estupido*! We want them in one piece!"

Fargo veered left, went forty yards, and veered right. He lost all sense of direction as he wound among the boles and thickets. The sisters never slackened, their ghostly faces bobbing with the rhythms of their mounts.

The forest was alive with Comancheros. To the north,

south, and east horses barreled through the vegetation and men questioned one another in Spanish and English.

"Have you spotted them?"

"Not yet."

"They went this way."

"No, this way."

Fargo reined up whenever he thought the cutthroats were getting too close. Twice he watched riders race past within a dozen yards of their hiding place. Chavez bellowed above the racket, issuing orders.

For twenty minutes Fargo played cat and mouse with the Comancheros. The sounds of crashing brush grew fainter and fainter, the yells tapered off. He gave himself a mental pat on the back for eluding them and turned to the sisters to let them know they were almost in the clear when to their rear a coyote yipped crazily. Only it wasn't a coyote. Now Fargo was certain that Comanches rode with the Comancheros.

Fargo threw up the rifle, but there was no one to shoot. A flick of his heels and he was off, galloping northwestward. At least he hoped it was to the northwest since the canopy overhead blocked the stars from view.

The chase was renewed. The Comancheros came on rapidly, sounding like a herd of buffalo smashing through the woods. And at their forefront, guiding them, the copper-hued coyote yipped steadily.

A hill rose out of the earth like a great dark belly. Fargo went around, picking his way with care among downed trees. The coyote was gaining, and when Fargo looked back, he glimpsed a vague form flitting through the trees. The Ovaro came to a high log and balked until Fargo jabbed his spurs. In a vaulting bound they cleared the obstacle and were in the clear.

Pausing to safeguard the women as they jumped over, Fargo was jolted at seeing not one but two wiry figures bearing down on them like human antelope. He sighted on the first, cocked the hammer, and stroked the trigger as delicately as he might a lover's nipple.

Thunder echoed across the woodland, and the lead Comanche spilled forward, hitting the earth with a thud. The second went to ground.

Both women had leaped the log. Fargo resumed riding, tossing the rifle aside. It only held one cartridge, and he didn't have ammunition. If the Comancheros caught them, he would fight tooth and nail.

Another coyote, his voice higher pitched than the previous one, led the Comancheros on the hunt. But this second warrior either was not as fleet of foot as his fellow brave or more cautious because he soon fell behind and his yipping ceased.

More hills poked skyward, Fargo threading among them at a reckless rate. A rare barren one stood out like a proverbial sore thumb. Fargo angled toward it, for from the top he would be able to get a clearer picture of the lay of the land and have a better idea which route was best to take.

A surprise awaited them. Fargo had no sooner stopped and turned the pinto so he could scour the area they had covered than Liberty pointed northward and thoughtlessly cried out.

"Look! A fire!"

Like a lighthouse beacon on the high seas, shimmering fingers of flame stood out in glaring contrast to the sable ocean of treetops. Fargo calculated the distance as two miles, possibly less.

"White men, you think?" Belle asked eagerly.

"Maybe Cull Holman and his bunch," Fargo said and smiled. With the guns of the old man's outfit to back them, they could hold off the Comancheros.

"What are we waiting for?" Liberty queried anxiously.

Fargo took the slope on the fly, with loud shouts ringing in his ears. Either the Comancheros had heard Liberty's yell, or they had been closer than he imagined. Baying like a pack of wolves, the killers swept through the forest to intercept them. "Go like hell!" he told the women.

All restraint, all caution, was thrown to the wind. The situation was critical; either Fargo and the sisters reached that beckoning fire or they would be recaptured. Fargo could have pulled ahead at any time, could have left the Boggs's to the cruel mercies of Caesar Chavez, but he remained at their side.

At breakneck speed their three mounts flew through the night. Limbs tore at them and tried to knock them from their saddles. Branches lashed their faces, their arms. Rocks clattered out from under the flying hoofs of their horses, making a spill a constant likelihood. But they rode on, dogged by human wolves the whole way.

Fargo knew it would be a near thing. They would reach the camp barely ahead of the Comancheros. Holman—if it was Holman—had to be warned or the Comancheros would tear through his men before they could unlimber their hardware.

When the campfire lay a couple of hundred yards off, Fargo rose in the stirrups and cupped a hand to his mouth. "Cull Holman! This is Fargo! I have the women, but the Comancheros are after us! Holman! Do you hear me!"

Men moved in the vicinity of the fire. Fargo kept on shouting, and in the woods they had just vacated Caesar Chavez was doing some shouting of his own, but Fargo didn't catch any of the words.

Like greased lightning they exploded from the forest into a long, wide meadow. At the far end flared the fire. The high grass brushed Fargo's boots as he leaned into the stallion's neck and raced flat out. Belle and Liberty were close behind.

Men in cowboy hats and vests were taking positions between the fire and the field. Fargo counted eight, all told, exactly as many as there should be in Holman's party if he had sent two hands back to Rawbone with the patent medicine man.

"Cull! It's me, Fargo!" Fargo bellowed one final time. "Don't shoot!" Glancing back, he saw the Comancheros pour from the trees in a ragged cluster. He guessed there were no more than fifteen, not the entire Comanchero band. Holman's men stood a chance.

A few more seconds and Fargo recognized Old Man Holman himself, pistol in hand. Beside him stood his son, Johnny, and Marshal Erskine. Fargo reined up almost on top of them and jabbed a finger at the riders closing in. "The Comancheros!" he declared.

For a man about to be confronted by the scourges of the territory, Cull Holman was remarkably calm. "No shooting!" he barked at his men. "Not unless I say so." Then he took a step to the left so he could see past the stallion and nodded at the sisters.

"Take cover!" Fargo urged, sliding off the stallion. "They'll mow you down if you don't."

"I don't think so," Cull said smugly.

Fargo was confused, and he wasn't the only one. Johnny and Erskine looked at one another. Belle and Liberty stared at the old man as if he was touched in the head. Even Holman's men appeared worried.

And then the Comancheros arrived, among them Little Mountain and two Comanches. Caesar Chavez was at the front. The Comanchero leader drew rein, pushed back his sombrero, nodded at Cull Holman, and shocked everyone by saying, "Hello, old friend! We meet again, eh?"

14

Skye Fargo recovered before any of the others. He remembered how the Comancheros laughed when Liberty proposed asking Old Man Holman to pay a ransom, and how at the time he had suspected there was more to their mirth than seemed apparent. How right he had been.

Cull Holman moved closer to Chavez and angrily gestured with his six-shooter. "Don't call me that, breed. We never have been friends and we never will be. All we have is a business arrangement that benefits both of us."

Chavez lost some of his sunny disposition. "Very well. We are business partners, then. But I must warn you, partner, not to call me by that name ever again. Several men have died for doing so."

Young Johnny Holman stepped to his father's elbow. "Pa, what is this? You know these vermin?"

"Hush, boy," Cull said. "I'll explain it all later."

"I want to know now."

"Hush, damn you!" Cull rasped and whirling, he slapped his son across his face. Johnny staggered but didn't go down. "This isn't the time to badger me with more of your silly questions."

Fargo grasped the Ovaro's reins and walked slowly past a stunned Erskine. He caught Belle's eye and wagged his head to indicate she should do the same. But when he tried to alert Liberty, she sat gawking at Holman and Chavez and didn't notice him.

The Comanchero leader had propped his hands on his saddle horn and was eyeing the younger Holman with amusement. "Do you mean to say, *Señor* Johnny, that your dear *padre* has never told you how he got so many of those nice things in your fine home?"

"No," Johnny said softly.

Cull Holman wore the look of a riled rooster about to unleash its talons. "You hold on, Chavez. This is a family matter and has nothing to do with you, so keep your big mouth shut."

"Ahh, but it does concern me," Chavez replied. "Your son called us vermin. Why? Because we barter in stolen goods? If that is the case, what does it make those we sell to? What does it make you?"

"You're prodding," Cull snapped.

Fargo handed the reins to Belle and, careful to make no sudden moves, retraced his steps. No one seemed the least bit interested in what he was doing. Holman's outfit were confused, not quite sure if they should regard the Comancheros as enemies or not. The Comancheros and Comanches sat impassively on their mounts, awaiting a cue from Chavez.

"I tell you, Johnny Holman," Chavez had gone on heedless of the father, "your *padre* has bought more from us than any other man I know of. Not so much of late, since he has his own town now and can afford whatever he wants. But back in the early days he took as many of the goods the Comanches brought back from Mexico as he could afford." Chavez sneered at Cull as if daring the lord of Rawbone to call him a liar. "This was before my time, but the way I hear it, he came here with a little money he had stolen, and he wanted to build a cattle herd. So he found the Comanchero camp and made a deal. Later he wanted more things. It did not seem to matter to him that people in Mexico were dying on Comanche raids so that he might have new horses or new furniture or—"

"Enough!" Cull roared. "By God, another word out of you, Chavez, and I'll plug you!"

Fargo had reached Liberty's horse and was leading it beyond the fire to Belle. All hell was going to bust loose, and he wanted to spirit the women out of there.

"Is it true, Pa?" Johnny Holman asked, his tone laced with horror. "Did you really deal with Comancheros?"

Marshal Erskine took a stride. "Tell us it ain't so, Cull. Tell me I haven't been working for a man who would let innocents die just so he could get rich."

Old Man Holman gnawed on his lower lip like a cornered rat. "Don't go jumping to any conclusions, boys," he said, forcing a smile. "Things were different back in them days. A

146

man had to get by any way he could. And once I had me all I'd ever wanted, I stopped dealing with these scum."

"God!" Johnny said in disgust. Turning away, he walked numbly into the shadows, head bowed in shame.

Erskine touched his left hand to his forehead. "I never should have left New Orleans."

"You don't understand, either of you!" Cull said sadly. "You weren't there, so you don't know how it was."

Several of the Comancheros chose that moment to laugh, among them Caesar Chavez. Cull Holman glanced up at them and something deep within him seemed to snap. Snarling like an enraged beast, he pivoted, raised his Colt, and thumbed off two shots that struck the Comanchero leader full in the chest, flipping Chavez backward off his mount.

For a fraction of a second the tableau was frozen as Comancheros and Holman's men alike gaped at the twitching body of Chavez, and then all of the Comancheros and Comanches came to life at once, slapping leather or lifting rifles. Holman's men already had their pistols out and began firing while scattering right and left.

Fargo witnessed all this while swinging onto the Ovaro. Since he didn't have a gun, he'd be no use in the fight. His first priority was to get the sisters to safety, and to that end he headed into the woods again, glancing back in time to see Marshal Erskine shoot a pair of Comancheros and in turn be blown off his feet by a blast from Fargo's own Sharps in Little Mountain's hands.

The foliage closed around Fargo, and he had to devote his attention to not being unhorsed by low limbs. For minutes the din of the battle raged. Guns boomed, men screamed and swore, horses whinnied in fright.

"Shouldn't we be helping?" Belle called out.

"And die on Cull Holman's account?" Fargo rejoined.

"But those poor cowboys!"

"Some of them might get away. Our main worry is Little Mountain."

"What do you mean?"

"If he lives, he'll come after you."

In silence they rode on, traveling mile after mile over the rolling hills, listening for pursuit that never materialized. Fargo was able to orient himself and set a course for Rawbone. Midnight came and went, and he cast about for a place to stop.

As they were negotiating a game trail that enabled them to make better time, the Ovaro bobbed its head and nickered. Fargo knew the signs and let the stallion go where it pleased. It left the trail, plowed through a row of low brush, and halted beside a sizable spring.

"How did you know this was here?" Belle marveled.

"Natural talent, I guess," Fargo answered with a straight face. Hunkering at the water, he cupped some and tested it with the tip of his tongue. A slight mineral taste was all he detected. "It's safe to drink," he announced.

And drink they did. Their lengthy flight across the Badlands and their race for life through the forest had left them parched and starved. The horses sank their muzzles in deep and guzzled noisily. Fargo went prone a few feet away, but drank only enough to satisfy his thirst. Too much, and he'd wind up with a wicked bellyache. He admonished the women to do the same.

Taking a seat beside a tree, Fargo rested, his eyes closed. Sleep pricked at his mind like a fingernail prying at skin, but he refused to give in. Not while the Comancheros might still be on their trail.

Liberty and Belle walked tiredly over and sank down next to him, one on either side.

"I don't mind telling you, Skye," Belle said, her face impish in the darkness. "I've been out with a few men before, but there isn't one who can hold a candle to you when it comes to showing a girl a good time."

Liberty giggled. "True enough, dear sister. Why, Mr. Fargo, here, about takes a girl's breath away."

"You're loco," Fargo said. "The two of you."

Both sisters rocked with laughter. Fargo opened his mouth to warn them to be quiet, then held his tongue. It had been a long time since they'd shared a hearty laugh. He put an arm around each of them and they rested their heads on his shoulders.

"Do you think Pa is still alive?" Liberty suddenly asked, spoiling the moment.

"We'll know soon enough," Belle said.

Fargo was about to offer his opinion when the Ovaro lifted

its head up from the water, ears pricked. He slipped his arms loose and held his palm out to Belle, who handed over the pocket pistol without an argument.

"What is it?" Liberty whispered.

"Don't know yet," Fargo said.

Moments later they all heard the sound of a horse coming toward them at a gallop.

"Little Mountain!" Liberty gulped.

"Quiet. And don't move." Fargo got a running start and vaulted onto the pinto from the rear. Snatching the reins, he rode through the brush to the game trail. Whoever was after them was making no attempt to ride quietly. He trotted to the wide bole of a forest giant and concealed himself behind it.

Soon the horseman appeared, whipping his mount madly. He wore no hat, and his long dark hair whipped in the wind.

A Comanchero, Fargo assumed, since the man wore clothes. The rider streaked around a bend and came to a straight stretch that passed the tree. Fargo sat motionless until the horseman was almost upon him, then he goaded the stallion onto the trail, blocking it, and aimed at the man's head.

"No!" the rider bawled. Hauling on his reins, he narrowly averted a collision. His horse pranced nervously as he threw out both hands. "Don't shoot, Trailsman! Don't you recognize me?"

Fargo had at the last second, which was the only reason Johnny Holman still breathed. "Did any of the others make it?"

"No, sir. Not that I saw, anyway." Johnny ran a hand through his hair. "It was terrible! Those bastards about blew Pa in half. Erskine had a hole in him the size of my fist. The rest fell one by one. I was the last, and I didn't aim to join them."

"How many of the other side were killed?"

Johnny patted his horse to calm it. "Everything was happening too fast for me to be sure, but I'd say eight or nine bit the dust and another two or three were singed." He mopped his face with a sleeve. "I never figured a gunfight would be like that. It was awful. All that blood and gore."

Fargo rested the pocket pistol on his leg. There was hope for the younger Holman after all, he reflected. "How did you know we came this way?"

"I didn't," Johnny said. "I was just trying to get away."

"Are the Comancheros after you?"

"They could be." Johnny's shoulders slumped. "To be honest, I didn't much notice. All I could think of was saving my hide." The young man stared off blankly into the trees and said forlornly, half to himself, "They killed my pa."

"So now you run the Holman empire," Fargo said, bringing the pinto next to Johnny's bay. "Has it sunk in yet?"

"Sure hasn't. I keep seeing my pa lying there in a puddle of blood and thinking of all the things he admitted before he died." Holman looked at Skye. "How could he have done it, Trailsman? You've rode the river a few times, I reckon. What makes a man do something like that?"

"He figured it was the right thing to do at the time. Just like you figured it would be fun to beat on Phinneas Boggs back in Rawbone."

"I didn't mean no real harm," Johnny said contritely. He seemed on the verge of tears.

"That was the boy in you," Fargo said. "And it's time for you to stop acting like a boy and be the man your father would want you to be." He nodded at Holman's Colt. "The Comancheros took my hardware. I'd be grateful if you'd lend me yours."

"Whatever for?"

"I'm sick to death of running."

"Sir?"

Fargo extended a hand. Johnny hesitated, glanced into the bigger man's eyes, and swiftly unbuckled his gunbelt. Fargo strapped it on, twirled the pearl-handled pistol out to check the loads in the cylinder, and shoved it back in the holster. "I'll drop it off when I reach Rawbone."

"You want me to go on by my lonesome?"

"No." Fargo pointed at the brush. "Belle and Liberty Boggs are hiding over there by a spring. You're to take them safely to town. Start now and don't stop until you tie your horse to a hitching post." He gave Holman the pocket pistol.

"What about you?"

"I have a score to settle." Fargo rode off, looking back only once. The young man was staring after him and waved. Fargo touched his hat brim as he went around a turn, then he doubled his speed.

The forest lay unnaturally quiet under the dim glow of a quarter moon. Animals and insects alike had been driven silent by the fury of the gun battle and the flight of the survivors. Fargo could have heard a pin drop, but he didn't hear the Comancheros or Comanches.

It was too much to expect they had given up, Fargo told himself. Either they were at the meadow, scalping and butchering the slain whites, or they had completely lost the trail and were miles away.

Finding the meadow proved more difficult than Fargo figured. The fire was harder to spot from the west, screened by dense trees. When at last he spied it, he was only half a mile away.

Boisterous voices and rowdy laughter resolved the question of the missing Comancheros. Fargo left the Ovaro in a stand of pines and cat-footed forward until the camp site and the atrocities being committed were indelibly branded into his memory.

No Comanches were to be seen. Seven Comancheros were alive, two of them wounded severely enough to keep them from the festivities. The other five were having themselves a grand time living up to their reputations as the most cold-blooded fiends on the frontier.

All the dead whites had been laid in a row and stripped naked. Their eyes had been gouged out, their fingers chopped off. Someone had seen fit to cut off a few private parts, as well. The Comancheros had soon lost interest in mutilating corpses and turned to live sport.

One of Holman's men had survived. Critically wounded in the chest, beaten bloody, he'd been deprived of clothes and tied to the tree nearest the fire. Gathered around him were the Comancheros, hooting and mocking him as one of their number carved into his chest with a butcher knife.

Fargo heard the man groan and edged closer. He saw a single dead Comanche sprawled in the meadow. Which meant Little Mountain and the other warrior were unaccounted for, a fact he didn't like one bit.

A scream of ungodly terror rang out. The Comanchero doing the carving had worked his way lower.

Lying in a pile on the far side of the campfire were the gunbelts and rifles taken from the dead men. Fargo made those his goal. From trunk to trunk he glided, moving as near as the vegetation allowed to the pile. The pair of wounded Comancheros sat with their backs to him while those watching the carving never bothered to look around. They believed the fight was over, believed they were safe to do as they pleased. They were wrong.

Fargo shucked Johnny's Colt and sprang into the open, his first shot jerking the knife wielder sideways with a hole where the upper ear had been. The next slug dispatched a Comanchero with hands like quicksilver; the man touched his twin pistols and died with a bullet through the nose.

In a frantic rush the rest broke for cover. One man raised a rifle and had his chest cored twice.

The wounded Comancheros leaped to their feet, one fleeing, one clutching at a revolver.

Fargo shot him in the face. There was a single cartridge left in the Colt, and he expended it on the other wounded man. Shots broke out as he dived and landed in front of the pile. From out of the jumbled belts and guns he grabbed a Remington. Flipping onto his back, thumbing back the hammer as he did, he prayed the pistol wasn't empty as he aimed at a stocky Comanchero trying to pick him off with a carbine. The Remington kicked, spitting smoke, and the Comanchero did a slow pirouette to the grass.

Jumping up, Fargo ran for the woods, bullets nipping at his legs courtesy of the sole remaining Comanchero. He gained the undergrowth and flattened. Slugs chipped off leaves and tiny branches overhead. Then the Comanchero's gun went empty and quiet reigned.

Fargo crawled to a log and slipped over it to the other side. He emptied the Colt and hurriedly slid six new shells from the gunbelt. While inserting the last one into the cylinder, he heard the crack of a twig to the north.

The last Comanchero was the impatient sort. Wearing greasy buckskins and a headband, he slunk along the tree line, availing himself of whatever cover was handy.

Lying still, left eye at the top of the log, Fargo held a pistol in each hand and let the hunter come to the hunted. A hint of fear lined the other's features, and Fargo could see beads of perspiration on the man's fleshy face.

The Comanchero stepped past a bush to a tree, but paused before ducking behind it.

Bending at the waist, Fargo leveled both arms as he surged upward, propping them on the log to steady his aim. He fired them simultaneously, the twin retorts like twin peals of thunder in his ears. The Comanchero reacted as if kicked by an invisible mule, flying over four feet and smashing into the trunk of an ash tree. Fargo fired again as the man slumped earthward and two holes blossomed on the Comanchero's shirt.

Fargo didn't move until the man stopped convulsing. Standing, he walked over, the pistols trained. He kicked the Comanchero's shoulder and the man tumbled.

Next Fargo ran to Holman's puncher. Unfortunately, the hand was dead. The wound alone would have been enough to kill him without the added grisly handiwork of the butcher knife.

Going from Comanchero to Comanchero, Fargo ensured each and every one shared the puncher's condition. On a thin man he recalled as being one of those always in Chavez's company he found his own gunbelt and Colt. They were soon about his waist.

There was little else Fargo could do. Lacking a shovel, it would take a full day to bury Old Man Holman's bunch, and he didn't have a day to spare. He did untie all the horses so they could graze. On a paint that had probably belonged to the same Comanchero wearing his Colt, Fargo came across his saddle.

It took under five minutes to bring the Ovaro to the camp and saddle up. Once aboard, Fargo felt almost complete again. The only items of his missing were the Sharps and the Arkansas toothpick, and if he was right, he could reclaim both at the same time.

A pink flush heralding the advent of dawn gave Fargo enough light to see by as he galloped into the forest. He was confident he could locate the spring again, and he did when the sun was an hour high.

The tracks told the whole story. Johnny Holman had done as Fargo wanted and gone to the sisters. Together they had taken the game trail as far to the northwest as it ran, then headed overland for Rawbone, still a day and a half off. Shortly afterward a new pair of hoofprints appeared, the prints of unshod horses. For over five miles the two riders had shadowed the unsuspecting young man and the women. Then, where a finger of prairie jutted into the woodland from the southwest, the pair had struck. The marks of a scuffle showed where Johnny, Belle, and Liberty resisted, but they had been overpowered.

Fargo gazed at the five sets of tracks leading southward. He hadn't come across any blood or a body, so the younger Holman might still be alive. Less than an hour's lead was all they had, and they would be moving slowly.

Once again the Ovaro was called on to give its all, and as always the stallion performed superbly. Fargo had those he was after in sight in under thirty minutes. They were strung out in single file, an Indian in front, an Indian at the rear, and were crossing a narrow valley bordered by a stream.

Fargo rode the high lines, keeping just below the rims so the Comanches wouldn't see his silhouette. He easily drew abreast of them, and from his roost he saw that all three captives were bound. Johnny had been dumped over his saddle and wasn't moving. Then he went on.

Dipping lower into timber, Fargo galloped toward the far end of the valley. He avoided rocky ground and anywhere else the pinto's hooves would make a racket. A gully filled with small yellow flowers brought him out where he needed to be.

There was only one problem. Other than the gully, he had nowhere to conceal himself. No trees grew within fifty yards, too far to risk a pistol shot. The grass wasn't high enough, either, not unless he lay down in it.

A brainstorm brought a grin to Fargo's face. He trotted up into the gully, going far enough so no one would hear the stallion if it whinnied. After securing the reins to a bush, he jogged to the bottom and into the grass. The Comanches weren't in sight yet, but soon would be.

Fargo had to guess at their line of travel and sank onto his side at an appropriate spot. Drawing the Colt, he bent stems over his body to blend him into the background. It was the best he could do, and three lives depended on it being enough.

Now came the hard part, the waiting. A bee buzzed by. Then a butterfly fluttered past. Fargo strained to hear the clomp of hoofs, but was disappointed. As time elapsed and they still didn't show, he wondered if perhaps they had changed direction and he was lying there like an idiot while they drew steadily closer to the Badlands.

Fargo's left ear, touching the earth, felt faint tremors before he actually heard the horses. The tremors became hollow drum beats, the drum beats the distinct thud of heavy hoofs. He had to resist an urge to sit and take a peek.

Presently the horses were so close Fargo could hear their breathing. He didn't think they could smell him, being as low to the ground as he was, but he tensed nonetheless when one of the animals neighed and all of them promptly halted.

Fargo envisioned Little Mountain studying the adjacent slopes, the gully, and the hills beyond the valley. The wily Comanche would be suspicious, but would keep on coming. And he would have a firmer grip on the Sharps—on Fargo's Sharps.

The hoofbeats resumed. A shadow flowed over the grass and enveloped Fargo. With utmost care he turned his head and saw the huge Comanche ten feet off, glancing warily around. Johnny Holman was next in line, wrists bound tight, his eyes open and betraying considerable pain. The sisters wore dejected looks of utter despair. Last in line was the other Comanche, a muscular warrior armed with an old flintlock.

Fargo curled his thumb on the hammer of the Colt and wished he had done so sooner. Little Mountain would go by within four feet of his hiding place and was bound to hear the click. He could see the Comanche's dark eyes darting every which way. Once they flicked past him and he tensed thinking he would be spotted, but Little Mountain failed to see him. The Comanche was concentrating on distant objects, not on the ground almost right under the hooves of his mount.

Then the moment of truth came. Little Mountain rode by and Fargo jumped to his feet, or tried to, his left leg becoming entangled in the grass and causing him to lurch to one side. He caught himself and straightened, but it was almost too late as the giant had whirled at the first sound and was bringing the Sharps into play. Fargo banged off two snap shots. Little Mountain's arms flew outward and he fell.

Turning, Fargo raised the Colt higher. The other Comanche was charging around the women, tucking the flintlock to his shoulder. Fargo aimed deliberately and fired once. In an ungainly somersault the warrior sailed off his mount into the grass. For a few seconds he was still, then he hooked an arm under him and tried to stand. Fargo took several steps, sighted, and put a bullet into the man's temple.

Accustomed as they were to gunfire, all the horses had stopped except Johnny Holman's. It nickered and began to flee. Fargo ran to its side and seized hold of its mane. "Whoa, there," he coaxed, hanging from its neck. "Calm down."

The horse pranced, but didn't try to rush off. Fargo released it and looked at Holman, belly down with the saddle gouging into his chest. "That must hurt," he said. "Here, I'll get you down." He slid the Colt into his holster and reached up.

Johnny Holman was looking at him in amazement, and suddenly Holman's eyes widened in fright and he found his voice, screeching, "Behind you!" At the selfsame instant, Belle and Liberty screamed.

Skye Fargo shoved backward from the horse and spun. The step saved his life as a Bowie knife cleaved the very space he had vacated. He stabbed for his pistol, but Little Mountain rammed into him, catching him across the ribs and lifting him bodily into the air. Fargo flew a few feet and jarred hard onto his spine. Again he grabbed for his Colt, but it had slipped loose when he was hit.

Little Mountain towered above him, two bullet holes marring the bronzed skin. One was high on the chest and would have finished off a lesser man. The other was close to the collarbone. The warrior's right shoulder sagged at an awkward angle, suggesting the shoulder was broken. In his left hand the giant clutched the Bowie, which he now drove at Fargo's throat.

Kicking with both legs, Fargo smashed his boots into Little Mountain's shins as he rolled. The Comanche grunted, nearly tripped, and the knife slashed wide of its mark. Fargo rose into a crouch, automatically going for the Arkansas toothpick in his right boot. Only it wasn't there. He'd given it to Liberty and had no idea where it was.

Bellowing like an insane bull, Little Mountain attacked, cutting wildly.

Fargo had to throw himself rearward and scramble to keep out of harm's way. He didn't realize he was retreating in a circle until he bumped into the warrior's mount. He tried to skip aside, too late.

Little Mountain slammed into him, nearly crushing Fargo's chest. Pinned, the massive weight of the giant grinding into him, Fargo just managed to lift a hand to block the descent of the Bowie. His other arm was held fast. They stood nose to nose, the Comanche straining to bury his blade, Fargo striving to hold it at bay. In the unequal contest the giant's strength began to prevail, the Bowie inching lower, steadily lower. The glittering tip was so close Fargo felt it prick his neck.

Suddenly, the Comanche's horse broke into a trot, throwing both men off balance. Fargo shoved as he stumbled to his knees and succeeded in hurling the warrior from him. The knife sought his heart and he jerked aside, landing on his right elbow.

For one so huge, Little Mountain was incredibly quick. He regained his footing and towered above Fargo like the living embodiment of his name. Fargo scrabbled backward to avoid several slashes. One clipped a whang off his buckskins.

Fargo scooted to the right, to the left. His outflung hand, seeking purchase behind him, touched cold steel. He probed, closing his fingers on a rifle barrel, its distinctive shape bringing a grim smile to his lips.

Little Mountain failed to notice. He only knew his quarry had paused, and with a grim smile of his own he stepped in close and prepared to deliver the killing stroke. His arm, as thick as a tree limb, swept high. He glared in triumph and hissed, "Now you die, white dog!"

"Think again, jackass!" Fargo said and saw the Comanche's eyes dart over his shoulder. The Bowie arced downward, but Fargo was already hurtling to the right, swinging the Sharps around as he did. At that range he didn't have to aim. He simply pointed the barrel at the warrior's head and fired on the fly.

Little Mountain staggered as the top of his forehead exploded. His arm sagged, he swayed like a mighty tree on the verge of toppling, then crashed to the earth with a loud thud.

Skye Fargo slowly stood, aware of the sun on his face and

the wind in his hair. He inhaled deeply, calming his nerves. That had been close—much too close.

Then a female voice jarred him back to reality. "Are you going to stand there all damn day admiring the flowers, handsome, or do you think you could find the time to cut us loose?"

the wind in his hair. He exhaled deeply, calming his horses.
That had been close —much too close.

"Excuse me," Belle called breathlessly from above. "Are you
...

15

Phinneas Boggs raised a bandaged hand off the bed and offered it to Fargo. "I can never thank you enough for all you've done. If not for you, my girls would be in the clutches of those horrible Comanches."

Fargo shook his hand lightly. "I hear you'll be back on your feet in another week."

The patent medicine man winked at his daughters. "With these two looking after me, sooner. They're enough to drive a man to drink with their nagging." He became serious. "Then I can get to work and put Johnny's sister on the mend."

Belle leaned down to kiss her father on the cheek. "That's my pa. Always thinking of others."

Touching his hat brim, Fargo walked out into the dusty street. He unwound the reins from the hitching post and stepped into the stirrups.

The sisters had followed him. Belle raised her hand in wistful farewell. "I hope that man in Texas understands about the delay."

"He will," Fargo responded. "I sent him a wire."

Liberty stepped to the rail. "You're a fool, Skye Fargo," she said bluntly. "You don't know a good thing when it's staring you right in the face."

The Trailsman gazed down the dusty street, out over the vast prairie, at the shimmering grass swaying in the golden sunlight. "Maybe so," he said, smiling, and with a nod he rode on out of Rawbone.

LOOKING FORWARD!
The following is the opening
section from the next novel in the exciting
Trailsman series from Signet:

THE TRAILSMAN #156
SAWDUST TRAIL

*1860, Oregon—just north of
the Rogue River, where death became
an echo of faraway places . . . .*

Skye Fargo's lake blue eyes were narrowed, his brow furrowed, as he peered at the turning, twisting road below. The coach traveling the road was unlike any he had ever seen before, a closed, high-roofed body painted entirely black with the driver seated high and forward. No Concord and no country brougham, not even a mud-wagon. It might have been a coupe with its low curving door and single window, but it had none of the graceful lines of a coupe. Everything about it was heavy, wheels wider, spokes thicker, the body bulky, almost cumbersome. Yet it took the uneven, twisting road with ease. He had been following it from the high hills most of the crisp fall day, and the driver was very good, very much in control of the two-horse team. Even the horses were unfamiliar, both rich chestnuts with bulging, broad forechests yet with a tallness that gave them grace as well as power.

But the coach was not the only thing he had been watching. A little after midday he had seen the five riders appear on the high land on the other side of the road, almost across from where he rode. They began to follow the coach, staying mostly in the mountain ash and the Rocky Mountain maple. Fargo's mouth grew tight as he watched the five riders. They were out for trouble. It was not just in the furtiveness of their movements, Fargo grunted to himself. He felt it inside himself, that sixth sense developed and polished with years of experience. They had doggedly followed the coach all afternoon, and now that the day began to slide toward an end, they began to move downward. The furrow slid across Skye Fargo's brow as he watched. The coach driver, intent on his driving, didn't see the five riders come down onto the road behind him, and Fargo took his horse downward along a shallow slope.

Below, the five riders were gaining ground on the coach, and suddenly the driver heard the sound of hoofbeats, turned, and saw his pursuers. He flicked his whip over the team and the horses surged forward, but the five pursuers had drawn their six-guns and were firing. Fargo spurred the Ovaro down the slope, his eyes on the scene unfolding before him. The driver tried to flatten himself on the seat and still keep his grip on the reins. He was somehow managing to keep control of the racing team and avoid the hail of bullets when two of the riders drew up on both sides of him. Their shots caught him in a cross fire, and his body turned and twisted on the seat before the reins fell from his hands and he toppled over the side of the coach.

A third rider dashed past to take hold of the cheekstrap of the nearest horse, and he slowly brought the team to a halt. Fargo continued to edge the Ovaro along the lower part of the slope, staying behind a thin line of hawthorns, and he watched as the five men dismounted alongside the halted coach. Two yanked the coach door open, and they pulled a tall, bearded man wearing a long coat with a fur collar from inside. He was apparently the only passenger in the coach, and he tried to fight back, but he was slammed to the ground. Fargo moved the Ovaro closer, still behind the tall hawthorns and saw the five men tear the clothes from the bearded man, his coat first, then a waistcoat and vest. They held him down as they stripped him of his trousers, and Fargo watched them search each item of clothing before discarding it. The frown dug deeper into his brow. This was no ordinary stagecoach holdup. They were plainly searching for something. Now down to his longjohns, the man was held on the ground by two of his attackers while the others threw the seats out of the coach as they searched inside the vehicle.

When they didn't find whatever it was they sought, they returned to the man and began beating him with kicks and vicious blows in between shouted questions. His lips a thin line, Fargo decided he had seen more than enough, and he reached down and drew the big Henry from its saddlecase as he moved the Ovaro farther downhill. He halted some twenty yards from the men, behind a thick shadbush just tall enough to screen him. He brought the rifle to his shoulder and fired, aiming his shot to slam into the ground inside the feet of a burly man who seemed to be the leader.

"That's enough," he called out as the bullet threw up a spray of dirt. "Get away from him."

The burly man straightened, surprise flooding his face as his eyes swept the hillside in the dusk. Fargo fired another shot into the same spot, and it threw up another spray of dirt. "Sure thing, mister," the man said and backed away from the beaten figure on the ground. The others followed his lead and backed away. The burly man peered up into the trees. "Come out where we can see you," he said. "We're not looking for trouble."

"You've a strange idea of being friendly," Fargo said, and his eyes swept the five men. They were ordinary enough in looks, the kind that could be hired most anywhere to do most anything. "Drop your guns," Fargo ordered. The burly one threw a quick glance at the others, and they spun as one, drawing their revolvers as they did, and sending a hail of bullets into the shadbush. Fargo dropped sideways from the saddle, the rifle in his hands, and heard the bullets whistle past him too close for comfort. He hit the ground, rolled onto his stomach, and aimed the rifle. The five men, crouched, were still spraying bullets in his direction, and he drew a bead on one, fired, and the man flew backward as his chest erupted in a torrent of red. He shifted the gun and fired again. A second man went down with a spinning motion. The others started to dive for cover, and one tried to climb into the coach. He was halfway through the doorway when Fargo's shot caught him. He pitched forward into the carriage to lay facedown with his legs dangling outside. They twitched for a moment before they lay still.

Excerpt from SAWDUST TRAIL

The last two had taken cover, one behind the coach, the other in a clump of aspen marked at the base by a row of ebony sedges. Fargo crawled downward on his stomach to halt behind a thin line of scrabble brush only a dozen yards from the coach. He let his eyes sweep the scene as the lavender of dusk began to deepen. The prone figure in his underwear groaned softly, but lay still, and Fargo swore under his breath. He hadn't a lot of time, the day waning quickly and the remaining two attackers playing possum, waiting for him to make an impatient mistake. Fargo decided the figure in the tree cover would be first, and he lay the rifle down and drew the big Colt .44 as he decided to make use of the trick a trapper had taught him. It depended on quickness of eye and marksmanship, and its success lay in triggering the automatic response that was part of animal and man.

He aimed the Colt at the ebony sedges, but as he pulled the trigger, his eyes were peering above the bullet's trajectory. He was ready as the shot plunged into the base of the sedges, the Colt raised as he saw the flash of answering gunfire from inside the aspen. He fired, two shots, and heard the gasp of pain and, seconds later, the thud of a body falling to the ground. "One to go," Fargo murmured softly as he peered at the coach. Dusk was sliding into night, and he inched himself forward on his stomach. Edging through the last of the brush as darkness descended, he halted, strained his ears, and heard the sound, footsteps moving quickly and lightly. He defined the form as it came around the rear of the coach, moving fast, dark against dark.

The man ran toward one of the horses, a blurry, indistinct target, and Fargo waited, his finger poised on the trigger, until the man pulled himself into the saddle. He was still for a moment, but a moment was all the Trailsman needed. Fargo fired and the figure toppled soundlessly from the saddle. Waiting a moment, Fargo pushed to his feet, picked up the rifle and trotted past the figure where a dark stain was already soaking into the ground. A moon rose to afford a pale light as he halted at the man they'd been beating and dropped to one knee. The man tried to sit up and gasped out in pain. "My body . . . it is broken," he said in a heavily accented voice, and Fargo helped

163

him to sit upright. "Slowly . . . slowly," he said as Fargo's hand pressed against his back. He had a strong face above the full beard, Fargo saw, a straight, prominent nose, heavy eyebrows and cheekbones, an imposing face with eyes that flashed dark blue fire despite his pain.

"Your driver's dead," Fargo said and the man groaned.

"Poor Svetlov," he said. "But I have you to thank for my life. *Spasibo, spasibo,* my friend."

"*Spasibo?* You're Russian?" Fargo frowned.

"*Da.* Yes. You know Russian?" The man frowned back.

"No, but I knew an oxcart driver who came from Russia," Fargo said. "He taught me a few words."

"I see," the man said as a shiver ran through him with a gust of sharp night wind. "*Poojalasta,* my coat," he said.

"I'd guess you have a few broken ribs at least," Fargo said as he helped the man slowly slip into his long, heavy coat.

"*Da,*" the man said as he steadied himself against the pain. "But I must go on. Others wait for me. You will be paid very well if you can take me to where I was going."

"Where's that?" Fargo questioned as he picked up the rest of the man's clothing.

"A place called Cornpipe, a road there they call Bear Trail. There is a house at the end of the road," the man said. "It will be worth your while, believe me."

"Why did those varmints attack you? What were they looking for?" Fargo questioned.

"It was a highway robbery. They were bandits," the man said, and Fargo held the smile inside himself. The answer was a lie. It had been no ordinary holdup. But his curiosity was aroused, and he never turned down the promise of good cash.

"All right. I'll give it a try," he said.

"*Khorosho.* Good. You have name, my friend?" the man asked.

"Fargo. Skye Fargo."

"Can you find this place by night, Fargo?"

"I make a living finding places. They call me the Trailsman," Fargo said.

"*Otchen khorosho.* Very good. I am Nicholas Rhesnev."

"What are you doing here, Nicholas?" Fargo asked as he put the seats back into the coach and tossed out the body.

"Visiting friends. Learning about this America of yours," Nicholas Rhesnev said as he climbed into the coach. Fargo smiled. It was another turn-aside answer, and he paused as his eyes held on the small lettering in white along the curved bottom edge of the door, five words written in the Cyrillic alphabet, and suddenly he knew why the coach was not like any he'd ever seen.

"You brought this coach with you," he remarked.

"*Da*," Nicholas Rhesnev said, pain in his voice. "A fine vehicle, made by Bulgannin in St. Petersburg, one of our best coachmakers. I felt Svetlov could make better time driving a coach he was familiar with."

Fargo's glance went to the tall, powerful pair of chestnuts. "The horses, too," he said.

"*Da*. They are what we call Dons, bred in the steppes of Siberia," the bearded man said. "But please, let us go. The pain is too much."

Fargo whistled and the Ovaro came at once as he climbed onto the driver's seat of the coach. The pinto would trot alongside, he knew, and he snapped the reins over the team. The coach began to roll, and he cast a passing glance at the bodies of the five attackers. All ordinary-looking, he concluded again. He'd find nothing by searching them. "I take it you don't want to bury your driver," he called back to the coach, leaning sideways from the seat.

"There isn't time," the voice returned, still full of pain, and Fargo sent the team forward faster. The horses responded quickly and handled beautifully, and he settled down to his driving under the moon that slid across the sky. He had never visited Cornpipe, but he knew it lay close against the western edge of the Umpqua forest, and he kept the horses driving northeast. The road stayed in mountain country, and as he drove, he heard an occasional moan of pain from the closed coach behind him. The bearded man's story about visiting friends in America was belied by the very coach he was driving, Fargo frowned in thought. One didn't bring over a coach, horses, and a driver for a leisurely visit to friends.

Nicholas Rhesnev had wanted his arrival to be kept secret. He wanted to avoid the talk that would accompany a foreigner buying a coach and team. But the plan hadn't succeeded. The attack had proved that. Why was secrecy so important, Fargo mused as he drove northward, moving into lower ground. The Russian team, the Don horses, were still responsive and showed no signs of tiring, he noted with admiration.

The moon was past the midnight sky, and he was traveling a wider road with rolling hills of canyon oak and quaking aspen on either side. The high moon afforded more of its pale light and, as normal as breathing to him, Fargo's eyes constantly swept the land on both sides and ahead as he drove. He estimated he had gone perhaps another ten miles and the moon was starting its downward path toward the horizon when he spotted a horseman at the edge of a line of canyon oak some fifty yards ahead. The rider began to move down the slope, and Fargo's eyes flicked to the opposite slope where he caught the movement that became two more riders moving toward him. No Stetsons or ten-gallon hats on them, Fargo noted. All wore close-fitting fur hats, and as they reached the road and started toward him, he snapped the reins hard and the two horses surged forward.

They would stay racing in a straight line, well-trained as they were, and he drew the Colt as he swung down onto the end of the long wagon shaft that ran between the two horses. Clinging with one hand to the shaft, the big rumps of the horses and the darkness all but hiding his figure, he saw the first two riders start to hold up when they saw no one holding the reins. His first shot caught the man on the left flush in the chest, and he flew backward from his horse. The second man to his right fired three shots, all too hasty as he searched to find his quarry. Fargo fired two back as he clung to the bouncing shaft. The first struck the man high in the shoulder, but the second tore into his midsection and he bent in two, clung to his horse for a moment longer, and then fell to the ground.

Fargo saw the third rider turn and streak away, and when the man disappeared, the horses had begun to slow their pace. Fargo pushed upward, swung his body in a backward arc, and climbed up onto the driver's seat. He took the reins and brought the horses to a halt, leaped to the ground, and went to the nearest of the two men. He stared up at Fargo out of lifeless eyes, but he was very different from the other five, younger, his face strong with high cheekbones, and he wore a shirt with a high, round collar that was definitely Russian. Fargo stepped to where the other man lay on his stomach and turned him over to see he wore another of the Russian shirts and the peasant trousers that went only to the knee. He stirred, and with his last breath muttered a handful of words in unmistakable Russian before his eyes closed for the last time.

Fargo strode to the coach and yanked the door open to see the bearded man in pain on the floor. He reached in and helped him up on the seat where he breathed long, harsh draughts, each one causing him to groan in pain. "These were no highwaymen," Fargo said. "These were your people, Russians. You want to tell me what the hell's going on?"

"Get me to the house, please. We can talk there," Nicholas Rhesnev said, and he wasn't faking his agony. Fargo closed the door of the coach and climbed onto the driver's seat. The moon had slid behind the hills as he sent the team forward, his eyes peering into the darkness, searching for the third attacker. The man hadn't just fled, Fargo was certain. He was out there someplace, perhaps waiting, perhaps following, but he was there. The first streaks of dawn stretched across the sky, and he kept the coach thundering along the road as the morning broke. Dark masses of shadow became oaks and piñon pines; great vistas of deep dark took form as rock formations, and he could see clearly now. But he saw no horseman waiting, no sign of the man who had fled. He slowed, halted at a stream to let the horses drink, and then went on toward the expanse of thick forest that rose up ahead.

Skirting the heavy line of white fir, hackberry, and mountain ash, he followed a well-worn road until the buildings of the town came into sight. A weathered road sign proclaimed its name: CORNPIPE, and he had almost reached the first buildings of what was plainly a small, ramshackle town when he halted alongside a man with two mules loaded with prospector's tools. "Looking for Bear Trail," Fargo said, and the man, small and stooped, pointed to the left.

"That way. Take the first cut on your right," he said and eyed the coach. "Don't know that your rig's going to fit," he said.

"Much obliged," Fargo said and sent the team to the left until he spied the first cut in the road. The prospector had been almost right in his guess, the coach barely able to take the narrow road. Tree branches hit against both sides of it as he moved down Bear Trail. The Ovaro fell back to trot along behind, and Fargo guessed he'd gone another mile when the trail widened slightly and he saw the house a hundred yards on, standing in a cleared patch of land alongside the trail. Two figures ran from the house as he drew to a halt in front of it with the coach, one a young man, tall, in a western shirt and dark trousers with a European cut to them, blond-haired with a clean-shaven face that would have been handsome except for a coldness in it and a cruel set to his mouth. The other figure was a young woman wearing a scoop-necked, yellow peasant blouse and a full skirt. She, too, was blond, a dark blond with her hair braided and the two braids worn up around her head. Fargo took in a very attractive face with broad, flat cheekbones, a straight nose, and a wide mouth with pale red lips. Brown eyes stared at him as the man strode to the coach.

"Where is Svetlov?" she asked, a faint accent in the words.

"Dead," Fargo grunted, and she frowned at once. She was about to ask him more when she turned her attention to where the young man helped Nicholas Rhesnev from the coach. Rheshnev, his face contorted with pain, just managed to walk toward the house with the young man holding him up, and the girl rushed to him, dismay clouding her face at once. Rhesnev spoke to her in Russian, and she raced into the house as the young man all but carried Rhesnev inside. Fargo stayed outside and leaned against the coach, and some ten minutes later she came from the house, hurrying toward him, and he watched the swing of full breasts under the blouse.

"Viktor is putting salve and bandages on his ribs," she said. "Nicholas told us what happened." She reached into a pocket in the skirt and brought out a roll of bills. "Here, fifty dollars. We are grateful for what you did." Her accent was less pronounced than Rhesnev's, but she carried some of his imposing face in her slightly regal manner.

"Keep it. I didn't do it for the money," Fargo said, and her eyebrows lifted. She studied his strong, chiseled handsomeness with a tiny furrow touching her smooth forehead.

"What you call a good deed?" she asked.

"What we call curiosity," Fargo said. "I'd like to know what this is all about."

The young woman's pale red lips pursed for a moment. "That is not for me to tell. Nicholas can tell you if he wishes to," she said.

"He owes me," Fargo said.

She thought for a moment. "Yes, perhaps he does, but that will be for him to decide," she said.

"Who are you?" Fargo questioned.

"Galina," she said, and a sudden smile made him realize that she was more than attractive, and that behind the air of regality there was warmth.

"Galina," he echoed. "I've never known a Galina."

Her brown eyes suddenly danced. "I'll wager you've known every other woman's name," she said.

"Enough," he conceded.

"I've been wondering where the handsome cowboys were. Now I've found one," Galina said almost mischievously.

"I've heard that Russian girls can be very beautiful. Now I know that's true," Fargo returned, and she laughed, a low, husky sound. His eyes stayed admiringly on her, his attention thoroughly on her, but like the mountain lion, a part of him was always aware of things around him, an inner sense always tuned to his wild-creature hearing. The sound struck his ears and took a half dozen seconds to translate itself, the stealthy rustle of leaves. *"Down!"* he yelled even as he tackled Galina around the waist and carried her to the ground beneath him as the two shots cracked through the air and he felt the bullets whiz past. He rolled from her, yanking his Colt from its holster, but he heard the sound of branches being brushed back. The attacker was running. "Get in the house," he flung at Galina as he leaped to his feet and raced to the Ovaro.

Vaulting into the saddle, he sent the horse charging into the line of canyon oaks. The fleeing figure was still on foot Fargo's ears told him, but he suddenly glimpsed a form through the trees as it leaped onto a horse. He swerved the pinto after the figure and saw the wool hat on the man, the third of the attackers who had fled. But not far, Fargo grunted with a kind of grim satisfaction at having been right. Being right had almost cost Galina her life, he realized as he took the Ovaro to the right of the fleeing horseman. The man's mount was having difficulty making time through the dense forest, Fargo saw, while the Ovaro's powerful hindquarters let it dodge and skirt trees with speed and agility. He was abreast of the man who turned, raised a pistol, and fired, the heavy bullet gouging a big piece of wood from an oak that the Ovaro skirted.

The man fired again, but as he spurred his horse forward, and his second shot went wild. Fargo wheeled the Ovaro and headed straight for him and saw the surprise on the man's face as he tried to fire another shot at the target that was now narrower. The surprise on his face changed to agonized pain as Fargo's shot caught him just below his rib cage. He pitched sideways from the horse as his mount spun, hit the ground, and was still before Fargo reached him. Fargo dropped to the ground and stared down at the man. He was definitely one of the last three, the round-collared shirt and a wide sashlike belt completing the Russian attire marked by his tight wool hat. If he needed more proof, it was in the revolver lying on the ground, a center-fire, single-shot piece of definitely Russian make engraved with scenes of battle.

He picked it up, pushed it into his belt, and swung onto the Ovaro. When he reached the house, Galina came running from the door and her arms were around him the moment he dismounted. "*Spasibo, spasibo,*" she said.

"The one that got away," Fargo said. "But not this time."

She stepped back, her brown eyes searching his face. "You are indeed very special, Skye Fargo," she said.

"Rhesnev told you my name." He smiled and she nodded. He handed her the pistol the man had held. "A gun from your country," he said.

"Yes." She nodded and pointed to writing at the end of the

ornately carved butt. "It is a *Tula* made by Goltiakov. He works for the Imperial Court. The engraving shows the defense of Sebastopol against the British and French."

"It's time for answers, honey," Fargo said grimly.

"Yes. Nicolas is bandaged and ready to talk to you," Galina said, and she took his arm as she walked to the house with him. She had a light but firm touch, and he found himself wondering not so much about the strange set of events that had taken place, but what he might learn about Russian girls.